BONVOYAGE

THEODORE AXEHANDLE

Artwork by
JAMIE C. SWEETIN

CABD
CONFORMANDBEDULL, INC.

Copyright © 2019 by Conformandbedull, Inc.

All artwork by Jamie C. Sweetin.

Published by Conformandbedull, Inc. (conformandbedull.com)

ISBN: 978-1-7332032-6-5 (paperback edition)

ISBN: 978-1-7332032-9-6 (e-book edition)

CABD
CONFORMANDBEDULL, INC.

For Jane, my constant love.

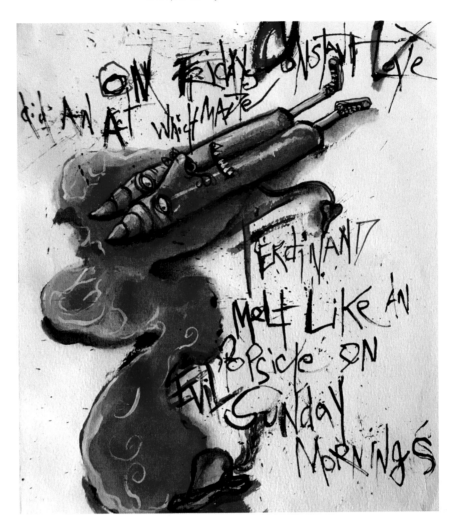

Taken

World! World! Let me out!
    See who darkness has taken.
    It spreads! Covering me in a blanket of ice.
    What is its use for me? I have but clothing and a twinkle of life.
    Its ruthless form devours everything in its path. My flesh is sparse.
    Make haste, my friends. Stale bread lies rotting on the floor.

— *Timothy Randolph*

CONTENTS

PROLOGUE

In the beginning, there was innocence. We swirled in the cosmic wondering as children of the universe. The universe kept us warm. We fed it the spirit and love that it lacked and for which it longed so deeply. From the chaos came harmony.

The rooting of our steel girders began with the first sprouting seed, its stems and leaves arching gracefully toward the heavens. Picture the sea, blue and simmering in its infancy; clouds, pink, settling above the horizon like the first sentinels, proud and erudite like mothers raining milk over the children teaming beneath them. Imagine the jungles and forests, a valley meandering among the sands and green hills.

That valley was Rockville. There held hands and formed communities. The communities elected leaders. And, rather than all having to meet at once, we let our elected representatives meet and speak for us — they were our voice.

The hoe carved its initials into the virgin earth. Rockville grew. It was discovered that the agrarian valley that helped to feed them could produce more if production was specialized. Such specialization required currency as a means of exchange, and then the currency itself became a commodity. With that production came mechanization, industrialization, and regulation. And factories. The factories multiplied.

The people of Rockville worked in the factories. They were much like us but slightly different in appearance — shorter and stouter. And some of them still dreamed.

In the heart of it all, Ferdinand was born — on the brink of disaster, on the brink of grey eternity, on the brink of growing up ... when his heart would no longer search the horizon for his lost innocence.

1

THE SPARK

Ferdinand was strung out. He would have given his little green hat and his sturdy leather boots for a deep puff of crackle — if he could find any. The caramel factory was running on alternating shifts of twelve hours per day and Ferdinand, being one of the few monitors of quality control for taste, color, and consistency, was required to work both shifts in a row, then off for twelve hours, then back to work.

He started the week on an intense high. He would rise early to delve into his crackle stash and spark the white crystalline rock until his head was brazen and electric, his eyes crazed, and his mouth chattering like a mad praying mantis. Throwing on his uniform, he would run wildly to the nearest Hinterland Station and catch the Corkscrew Rail into downtown where the smeltery stacks hissed and coughed their foul brew high into the sky, the smoke twisting and coiling through the tortured rail above him. By Friday, however, he had used the last of his precious rock, and the double shifts were taking their toll.

The waning moments of the workweek only exaggerated Ferdinand's exhausted condition. He was focused heavily on the knowledge that he would soon have a bag full of coins and, for the first time in over two months, two entire days to wind down ... and smoke some crackle.

When the factory whistle finally blew, Ferdinand punched the clock and grabbed his black overcoat. All around him, the caramel machines were steaming and chugging to a stop like a carnival symphony. Moving into line, he began the slow herd walk to the exit and on to his box stop on the Corkscrew Rail.

Altruistic Joe walked up behind him. "Hey, Ferdinand, you heading to the Jalapeño Lounge? A few of the guys from work are going over, and Weasel's supposed to be bringing some crackle."

Altruistic Joe was one of the nicest guys Ferdinand had ever met. A.J. had only recently started smoking crackle and just now his eyes gleamed with it.

"Look, A.J., I'd love to, but you know I can't stand Weasel Salsa. He's such an asshole!"

"Yeah, but he's got crackle," countered A.J. "Anyway, a lot of the guys are going over. Just grab a beer if you want. Abbot will be there!" he pointed out.

Ferdinand acquiesced. After all, Weasel was bringing crackle and the Jalapeño Lounge was one of his favorite nightclubs. Furthermore, on Friday nights Constant Love put on a show that made Ferdinand melt like an evil Popsicle on a Sunday morning. "All right, A.J. What the heck!"

The Jalapeño Lounge was on the south side of Rockville, about twenty blocks from the caramel factory. It wasn't a great area, but it wasn't as crime-ridden and generally bad as Barnacle Row either. Even though the tuffies still patrolled it, their presence was sparse.

The two friends, still draped in their stinky burlap work garments, walked the few blocks from the Southside Station to the lounge through a series of warehouses, carefully keeping an eye out for any lurking danger.

As they approached the Jalapeño Lounge, they noticed Constant Love going in through a side door. "She's so damn hot!" exclaimed Ferdinand.

Overhearing him, Constant Love turned to look. She was undeniably beautiful. She possessed an olive complexion, green eyes, and long, flowing auburn hair. Constant Love was tall, standing nearly four feet, and maintained a calm, smoldering demeanor. She flashed Ferdinand a sardonic smile and then slipped into the building, the door closing behind her like a loyal servant.

"Give it up," came Abbot's voice from the front door of the lounge. "She's trouble with a capital T, my man. Besides, B.S. Hun would kick the living shit out of you if he caught you writing a love ballad with *that* one."

Ferdinand sighed. Abbot was right, of course, but just for once he'd like to taste the good life.

"Ferdinand!" Abbot called out. "You coming in or am I going to have to lead you by the dick?"

Ferdinand snapped out of his self-absorption and walked into the bar with A.J. The Jalapeño Lounge was dark, as usual. A long, metal bar extended along the length of the southern wall in the shape of the pepper from which the lounge took its name. The décor was similarly consistent, painted in dark greens and reds and partitioned with stained, thick curtains.

The three friends lined up on consecutive stools at the bar. The bartender, a reputed member of a local gang called the Gremlins, sauntered over from the coin safe. "Gents," he said. "We're running a special on crackle, if any of you are interested."

"Crackle! Shit!" exclaimed Ferdinand. "I thought crackle was illegal!"

"It is," said the bartender. "Do you want some or not?"

A.J. addressed the opportunity. "Ya, I'll take some."

"Well, no shit! Crackle all around, my man!" declared Ferdinand.

The bartender brought out a pipe, a book of matches, six chunks of crackle, three beers "on the house," and two bowls of caramels, individually wrapped. "That'll be ten coins," he said.

"No problem," replied A.J. as he counted out ten coins on the bar.

"A.J., how much do you spend on crackle a week?" asked Abbot.

"I don't know," said A.J. "How much do you spend?"

The three were silent. Ferdinand reached over and grabbed the pipe. His thick hands wrapped around the cold metal like a coiled snake. He lit the bowl and sucked in deeply. The white metallic flavor basted his tongue, throat, and lungs with a sour, invigorating nausea of pleasure. He handed the pipe to A.J. and grabbed some caramels. Having unwrapped four or five, he smashed the caramels into a sticky ball and bit into the center as if it were a candied apple.

"Damn, Ferdinand! Don't you ever get tired of caramel?" asked Abbot. "I mean you eat the shit all day long! How can you sit there and stuff a giant ball of caramel into your mouth?"

"It's free," Ferdinand suggested. "I like it. Besides, what do you care?"

Abbot just sat there looking at him. A.J. was sucking on the pipe.

"Let me know when you want a real meal and it's on me, okay?" said Abbot.

"All right," Ferdinand agreed as he sunk his stained, sticky brown teeth into the caramel again.

It was still early. At least an hour would pass before Constant Love would take the stage, so they decided to pass the time by watching the electrovision behind the bar. It was showing an address by the Headmaster Hedonist. Ferdinand, who was getting anxious waiting, asked the bartender to turn up the sound.

The Headmaster Hedonist was making his quarterly address directly from the Abomination House. He was dressed in crimson robes with a large silver cone decorating his crown. His eyes were shaded like a bandit, and he held a great metal-studded club that he used to strike a big circular gong to his left to accentuate his points.

"I am going to crush the infidels [*gong!*] and reestablish the hierarchy of values within our tenements. [*gong!*] Never before has such a slithery sliding scale of demonstrative destruction destroyed our children. [*gong!*] Heretofore, I shall resurrect [*gong!*] a landmark [*gong!*] for joyous occasions. [*gong!*] A new war on crackle shall be implemented within our ranks. [*gong!*] And I shall quell the interlopers with the power of my hand. [*gong! gong! gong!*]"

Ferdinand looked over to Abbot, who was busy taking puffs off the pipe. He paused a few moments, then turned his attention to A.J., who hadn't heard a word of the speech and was busy scraping caramel off the bottom of his boot. Ferdinand, who had thought the speech contrived and patronizing (and who was hoping for a concurring spark of recognition in the expression of his friends and finding none), elected to focus his attention on the stage where Constant Love was due to be making her appearance. In so doing, he spotted Big Stick Hun sitting at a table near the stage.

Not only was Big Stick a blatant crackle user, he was also a major crackle *dealer*, an underworld thug, and the founding member of the Gremlins. Big Stick had an unparalleled reputation for madness. Even so, Ferdinand had more disgust than fear when it came to Big Stick Hun. The fact that he was Constant Love's main squeeze sickened and angered him. He couldn't understand what such a beautiful woman could see in a repulsive monster like Big Stick.

Feeling Ferdinand's eyes on him, Big Stick turned and gave Ferdinand a cold, hard stare. Ferdinand looked at his friends, one on either side of him. "Fuck!" exclaimed Ferdinand. "What is his problem?!?"

The three sat there shaking their heads and muttering into their beers. A.J. sucked on the pipe and ordered another round from the bartender. All the while, the bartender was staring out of the corner of his eye at Big Stick Hun.

Abruptly, the lights went down in the bar and the curtains to the stage opened. Constant Love took the stage. Ferdinand could hardly blink. She mesmerized him. He had never seen a woman so exotic, yet soft in her movements. Constant Love was stunning. She was dressed in a red satin, full-length gown that stuck to her like an eighth layer of epidermis. The pattern on the gown reflected a series of interwoven hearts, each one a window to her heavenly flesh. She was radiant under the lights of the Jalapeño Lounge.

Constant Love began to dance on stage. She was writhing and twisting beneath the red lights like a serpent possessed, slithering to the sounds of chugging bongos. Her legs stretched, her back arched, and her fingers wound around her body. The dance was freedom and independence personified. She pounced and rolled and mouthed the word *bonanza* over and over to the rhythm of the bongos. All the while, her eyes remained fixed on a frozen, mesmerized Ferdinand.

For the past two months, Ferdinand had been treading water in a relationship with his new girlfriend, Penelope. Penelope was a loving, steady, affable young woman. She had initially pursued Ferdinand with the will of a woman thirsty for motherhood, having found him more than adequate for the position. Ferdinand, not used to the flirtations of the opposite gender (and never having been one to visit the supermarts where the girls charged for bonanza), was flattered by Penelope's early attention and often stoked its flame. Moreover, they each had steady jobs and bright futures. But Penelope wasn't Constant Love and, while the opposite also held true, Constant Love held Ferdinand in her lusty grip.

So, Ferdinand kept staring at Constant Love as if in a trance. She was openly cognizant of the attention and clearly enjoyed it. Big Stick Hun was cognizant of the attention as well and was sending Ferdinand short, electric messages of danger that were simply not being received.

"Ferdinand," Abbot barked, trying to shake his friend out of his stupor. "Don't you think maybe you'd better check out the electrovision again?"

"Huh?" asked Ferdinand, turning his attention toward Abbot.

"Just go back to watching the speech, Ferdinand," he continued. "Don't forget who's sitting in the audience."

"Oh, yeah. Right," Ferdinand mumbled, aware now that he had not only sparked Big Stick's attention, he had ignited it. Ferdinand turned his back on Big Stick and Constant Love and focused his gaze on the electrovision. "The speech is over," he noticed out loud.

Ferdinand caught the reflection of the stage in the mirror behind the bar. Big Stick had climbed onto the stage and was grabbing Constant Love by the shoulders, maniacally jamming his thick tongue down her throat in a primitive display of power and control. Constant Love was struggling and kicking to break free of his grasp whereupon Big Stick knocked her to the floor with a broad slap across her face. Constant Love scrambled to her feet and darted backstage.

Big Stick jumped off the stage and returned to his table, joining his fellow Gremlins who were all staring directly at Ferdinand and his two friends.

Abbot and A.J. started yanking on Ferdinand's sleeve, with A.J. pleading for them to get out of the building.

To their horror, Big Stick suddenly pulled out a submachine gun, screamed "Bon-voy-age!" and started raining bullets indiscriminately across the lounge. Metal sparks popped and flashed as fragments of the bar burst free all around them.

Ferdinand, Abbot, and A.J. jumped behind the bar, crouching behind the metal jalapeño-shaped barrier.

With that, Big Stick pulled out a hand grenade and swiftly chucked it behind the bar.

"Shit!" Ferdinand yelled, scrambling to retrieve the grenade. As quickly as he could, he grabbed the weapon and threw it through a swinging door behind the bar.

The grenade exploded, blasting the swinging door from its hinges altogether. Splintering pieces of wood drove into the bartender's leg, who was crouched behind the bar with them. The bartender screamed in pain.

"He's got a problem," A.J. mentioned halfheartedly, as he pulled a crackle pipe from his pocket and took a puff.

"A.J., put that goddam pipe away!" yelled Abbot.

"There is no god," commented Ferdinand.

At that exact moment, unaware of the havoc inside, Weasel Salsa stomped into the bar and shouted, "Crackle for everyone!" with his arms raised high in the air, bags of crackle hanging from each hand. Weasel didn't seem to notice the goings-on inside the lounge until Big Stick started firing madly in his direction. Weasel quickly jumped over the bar with the others.

Hiding behind the bar, their breathing now heavy with anticipation, they heard the heavy, methodical footsteps of Big Stick lumbering toward the makeshift barricade, approaching their place of refuge. Abbot was frantically looking for a way out when he noticed the bleeding bartender crawling through an opening in the wall behind the bar. Abbot grabbed Ferdinand and the two began crawling through the same opening, which appeared to lead to the alley outside. As they reached the opening, Big Stick jumped on top of the bar and fired a short blast, missing high over their heads.

A.J. and Weasel seized the opportunity to race for the front door. Big Stick noticed and started firing blindly, scattering bullets in a 360-degree blast around the room. Weasel and A.J. tumbled through the front door of the Jalapeño Lounge and disappeared into the night.

Abbot and Ferdinand escaped through the back opening of the

Jalapeño Lounge and into the alley and the transparent safety of the shadows of the outlining buildings. They could still hear gunfire echoing from within the lounge.

Ferdinand couldn't help but wonder if Constant Love was still alive.

Glancing back, Ferdinand could see Big Stick and three Gremlins exit the lounge, firing back into the building as they went.

"Abbot, that's him," said Ferdinand. Abbot didn't look back, but kept running. Ferdinand and Abbot continued to distance themselves from the lounge. They hurried around a corner until they came to rest under the soft illumination of a streetlamp.

"Uh, Ferdinand, I hate to tell you this, but you're bleeding," said Abbot.

Ferdinand looked over his body and saw that his burlap baggies were saturated with blood around the area of his left thigh. "I must have been shot," said Ferdinand.

"That's good," replied Abbot. "At least we know your brain is working. You might want to check that out, Ferdinand."

Ferdinand leaned over his left leg and felt the wound with his hands. "I think I just got scratched," he said.

"Good. Let's go," said Abbot.

The two walked through the maze of warehouses surrounding the Jalapeño Lounge in hopes of distancing themselves from the Gremlins and eventually reaching the Corkscrew Rail.

"We need to get you to a morgue," said Abbot. "You're bleeding pretty bad."

Ferdinand agreed but didn't feel the wound was life-threatening. The heightened state of fear was foremost in his mind. It seemed as if they would have to walk across the entire length of the Outlands before reaching the Southside Station. The further they got from the Jalapeño Lounge, the darker the streets became. The streets smelled of metal and grease. The boys zigzagged between the large warehouses, peering around corners and staring into the black before proceeding. They each looked behind the other. They each looked side to side. They slowly wound their way toward the Southside Station.

Eventually, they came to hear the sounds of the rolling track. They could hear the chain chugging the cars to the top, where they would split off from the main line toward the separate provinces of Rockville, the cars whipping down and around the track like the wind. Finally, they could see the lights: first, lights from the top of the tall rail itself, appearing like strung lanterns; then the lights from the Southside Station, just ahead of them.

They increased their pace as they headed toward the entrance of the station, Ferdinand now skipping straight-legged toward the rail. As they reached the end of the last warehouse, they peered across a flat, open cement area over which they would have to cross to reach the platform entrance. They searched for Gremlins and saw no one, save a car full of tuffies patrolling up the street to the west. They stayed to the shadows and kept going.

Just as they reached the halfway point, Big Stick and two Gremlins jumped down from a platform and jogged toward them. Big Stick was carrying a mace, which he began to swing violently in a circular motion as he ran toward Ferdinand.

"Fuck!" Ferdinand yelled.

Ferdinand and Abbot turned to run back toward the warehouses when they saw another Gremlin running up at them from behind. They turned again and took off, but Ferdinand was hobbling badly. The Gremlins were quickly gaining on them. To make things worse, that car full of tuffies had again pulled into view, tires burning against the cement as the car came screeching down the road, directly toward them.

Big Stick reached Ferdinand first. He swung the mace wildly, hitting Ferdinand on the neck and head. Ferdinand fell to the ground, knocked unconscious.

Big Stick dropped the mace and pulled a hatchet from his boot. He raised the hatchet in a crazed attempt to cut off Ferdinand's head.

Meanwhile, the car full of tuffies had screeched to a halt and one of the tuffies stepped from the car. The tuffie pointed a pistol-gripped shotgun at Big Stick and ordered him to drop his weapon.

Big Stick stared at the tuffie while slowly placing the hatchet back into his boot and picking the mace up off the ground. As Big Stick turned to walk away, one of the tuffies gestured for him to get into the car. He did.

The patrol car sped away with Big Stick while the remaining Gremlins walked off, leaving Abbot and Ferdinand alone in the street.

Abbot took off his shirt and tied it around Ferdinand's head. He picked up his friend, who was still unconscious, and carried him the remaining distance to the Corkscrew Rail. From there, they took the rail to the nearest morgue — the Homestead Morgue in southern Rockville.

As he lay unconscious in the railcar, Ferdinand found himself underwater, playing in the heavy blues of the deep ocean like a dolphin. He swam to the surface and leapt over barriers of barbed-wire fence. His teeth were knives and they gleamed in the midday sun as he jumped above the water. Constant Love was a cloud, and she rained glycerin and honey from her eyes over his smooth skin and into his mouth. He flipped up and grabbed her, and they landed in green fields, beyond Rockville, in a place beyond the Outlands called Bonvoyage.

2

THE FUSE

When Ferdinand woke up, he saw the outline of a figure in front of him. He felt a hand gently caressing his forehead and petting his hair, which was falling in front of his eyes.

"Ferdinand, it's me, Penelope," she said.

Ferdinand looked up, attempting to focus.

"Ferdinand," Penelope repeated.

He struggled to focus as Penelope slowly came into view.

"Hi, Ferdinand. Welcome back," she said.

"Oh, hi," said Ferdinand.

"How are you feeling?" Penelope asked.

"All right, I guess."

Ferdinand noticed that the electrovision in the corner of the room was on and showing an address by the Headmaster Hedonist. "What's that?" he asked.

"Oh," said Penelope. "That's the Hedonist talking about the crackle problem. He's been on nonstop for nearly 24 hours now. A lot of people think he's on crackle. Anyway, after what happened at the Jalapeño Lounge, *The Slanted View* ran an article about it and I guess one of the Malevolent Seven from Rockville started blaming the Hedonist's policies. So, the Hedonist has been on the E.V. ever since."

"Twenty-four hours? How long was I out?" asked Ferdinand.

"Oh, at least a couple of days, Ferdinand," answered Penelope.

Ferdinand sighed and gently shook his head. "Turn it up for a second."

Penelope walked over to the electrovision and turned up the sound. The Headmaster Hedonist was dressed in bright orange robes tied at the waist by a thick, red rope. His eyes were again covered like a bandit and he held a large megaphone through which he was speaking.

"I repeat," the Hedonist said. "I have never, and will never —"

Before he could finish, the electrovision suddenly went blank.

"What's that about?" inquired Ferdinand.

"I have no idea." She paused. "You know some people consider him a genius," said Penelope.

"Really," said Ferdinand, caustically.

Just then a technician entered the room and began reading Ferdinand's chart. He looked up and said, "Well, I see that you're awake. You know, Penelope, you really should have informed us."

"I know, but he seemed okay, and we were just talking," Penelope explained.

While the technician examined Ferdinand, Abbot entered the room wearing white robes and sandals. "Hey, Ferdinand, I brought you some crackle," he announced.

"What the ..." stumbled the technician. "Look, what you do on your own time is your own business, but in here, *we* administer the crackle. He's been on a crackle saline solution, in controlled doses, for over two days, to help electrify his brain waves. Any more might make him topple, if you know what I mean. So, please, let us administer the medicine, will you?"

"All right. Anyway, I was only playing around. I don't do that shit anymore," said Abbot, as the technician left the room.

"What do you mean?" asked Ferdinand.

"I mean I don't smoke that fucking shit anymore, that's what I mean," said Abbot.

"What are you talking about?" Ferdinand asked.

"Look, Ferdinand," said Abbot. "A lot has happened since you were under. I've been listening to the teachings of The Man With No Name, and he makes a lot of sense, you know? I mean, what are we doing every day ... just working at the caramel factory? I mean, *sure* we make caramel — that's good. But, what does it accomplish? Why are we here, Ferdinand? I'll tell you why we're here. To do The Man With No Name's work, that's why, and that doesn't include doing crackle."

Ferdinand stared at Abbot. "What are you wearing?" he asked.

"I'm wearing robes, Ferdinand. You know, something other than a goddam ... oh, sorry, something other than a fucking burlap sack, man. I'm sick of baggies. Besides, these robes really reflect the light."

Ferdinand stared at Abbot, speechless. All of a sudden, the electro-vision clicked back on. The Hedonist was lying naked in a bed of flower petals.

"Let us review," said the Hedonist. "I am in control. I have listened to The Man With No Name, and I know his teachings. When we play upon the madness of the soul, we play a ballad, but when we desire to pluck the tulips from the ground, we plant the seeds of industry. In my term as Headmaster Hedonist, I shall industrialize within the goodness of the soul and turn the tide against Salamander Meeks and his evil snot-dripping crackle."

Ferdinand sat up, leaned forward, and started to vomit. Penelope rushed over and held his hair back while Ferdinand threw up on the bed. He was breaking out in cold sweats. "Shit, sorry," he said. "I don't know what's the matter with me."

Penelope ran to get some assistance while Abbot helped Ferdinand lie back down. "Look, Ferdinand. You may not believe it, but The Man With No Name is right. He's seen the light. He knows, Ferdinand. He knows why we're here and why we do the things we do and why we don't do the things we don't do, you know?"

"I don't know what you're talking about, Abbot," said Ferdinand. "I mean, what are you talking about? We almost got killed, *The Slanted View* runs some article about all this, the Hedonist is on the E.V. blabbering about who knows what, and you're a ... well, I don't know what you are."

"That's just it, Ferdinand," replied Abbot. "The Man With No Name knows! He will plant the seeds in the coming age to dissolve the power and evil of Salamander Meeks."

Ferdinand sighed. "I'm so tired," he mumbled to himself. "I don't know what's up or down anymore. I had this dream. There was this place — a lot better place ... Bonvoyage. It was beautiful."

Abbot reached forward and handed Ferdinand a copy of *The Slanted View*. "Look! Bonvoyage! I saved the paper for you — it's the first article.

Ferdinand picked up the paper and began to read.

Destruction. Death. Bullets. More Death. Bonanza. All mixed together like a bad headache medicine last night at the Jalapeño Lounge. B.S. Hun, a reputed Gremlin and crackle fiend, screamed "Bonvoyage!" before killing 14 with a submachine gun in a raging terror. The scene was one of pure death.

"I've never seen anything like it," said Mack "Weasel" Salsa, a local boy from the caramel factory. Indeed, the death toll from last night's onslaught bumped the Southside homicide rate through the clouds, topping last year's record-setting numbers.

The motive behind last night's shooting rampage remains unclear, although certain witnesses have indicated that B.S. Hun was enraged over the recent quarterly address by the Headmaster Hedonist, which was showing on the lounge's electrovision immediately before the shooting.

The Jalapeño Lounge, reputed for its star entertainer, Constant Love, may never be the same.

"It may never be the same," commented Constant Love.

Meanwhile, B.S. Hun remains at large while a Rockville manhunt searches for this master of disaster.

"She's alive," thought Ferdinand.

Penelope walked back into the room with a helper who immediately began to clean up Ferdinand's vomit.

"You're one sick motherfucker," said the helper. "I haven't had to clean up someone's vomit in years. What did you go and vomit for?" she asked.

"I don't know," replied Ferdinand. "Sorry."

"Well, don't do it again on *my* shift."

"Ferdinand's always been a little high strung," said Penelope.

"I have not!" Ferdinand appealed. "What did you say that for?"

"I'm not getting involved here," interjected the helper. With that, she grabbed the vomit-stained sheets and the little pail of Ferdinand's vomit (which appeared to be mostly caramel) and left the room, shaking her head in disgust.

"Ferdinand," said Penelope, as she took a crackle pipe from her waist bag. "Don't start asking *me* questions. What were you doing at the Jalapeño Lounge?" Penelope lit the pipe and puffed deeply, her cheeks expanding from the vile gas.

"I was meeting some of the guys," answered Ferdinand. "It was Friday night, okay, and I needed to unwind. Shit, I've been working double shifts for the past two damn months, Penelope!"

"Don't you swear at me, Ferdinand. You're the one that almost got killed because you were frequenting that sin din. Serves you right for fornicating like that."

"Serves me right?!?" exclaimed Ferdinand in disbelief. "All I was doing was drinking a beer and smoking a little crackle. Then Big Stick Hun went fucking berserk. What are you talking about, serves me right? Give me a puff of that."

Penelope handed him the pipe. "Well, all I know is that you didn't call, Ferdinand. You were out staring at Constant Love and I was home smoking crackle by myself."

"Look, you two," threw in Abbot. "There are more important things than ourselves. You have to start thinking about your souls. Who will protect your soul when it's bathed in crackle?"

Ferdinand sucked in deeply and nearly passed out. He blew out a noxious white cloud of smoke, coughed, and handed the pipe back to Penelope. Ferdinand looked at Abbot. Abbot was staring at Ferdinand with a grim expression. Ferdinand could take it no longer and started to laugh. He laughed for a full five minutes as Penelope and Abbot watched him, growing more concerned by the minute.

"I think he needs psychiatric help," said Abbot.

Penelope just stared at Ferdinand ... and worried.

Ferdinand was slowly descending from his cloud and back into Rockville when Weasel Salsa entered the room. "Hey, Ferdinand, what's up?" greeted Weasel.

"Nothing's up, Weasel. I'm lying here from an apparently serious head injury and my leg's bandaged. Get it?"

"Gee, sorry, Ferdinand," offered Weasel. "Sorry for that ... ya ... hmmm. Ya, you know I've never been shot, that's true. Sorry about that, Ferdinand."

"What do you want, Weasel?" demanded Ferdinand.

"Oh. I just wanted to see if you were okay, ya know."

"That's nice," said Ferdinand.

"Look," said Weasel. "You didn't happen to see anything peculiar at the Jalapeño the other night, did you?"

"Peculiar?" queried Ferdinand. "You mean like a gun-toting wild man on a death rampage?"

"No, you know, like maybe something in the back room. Large bins of crackle, anything like that?"

"No, Weasel. Nothing like that," said Ferdinand. "Besides, that room was pretty much coals when I left."

Meanwhile, Abbot was staring out the window, crying. Penelope was brushing away his tears and comforting him.

"Well, fuck!" exclaimed Weasel. "You know, you do somebody a favor and you get fucked. Remember that, Ferdinand."

"I don't know what you're talking about, Weasel."

"I'm talking about how I got fucked," said Weasel. He sighed and sat down on the edge of the bed. "Fuck!" he bellowed again. Weasel was beside himself. "Look, Ferdinand, you were my last hope. I was talking to the bartender one night at the Jalapeño and I was telling him about how I knew this guy, one of the tuffies who had this connection. I don't know where he gets it, if it's from people he shakes down or somewhere else, but he's got an endless supply of crackle. Anyway, I've been selling a lot, as you may have heard, and I thought I'd cut the Jalapeño in on a little business deal. Well, before Big Stick shot the place to hell, there was a large deposit of crackle. Anyway, those fucks cut me out! Big Stick, all those fucks! I'm out. They're dealing directly with this tuffie."

"I thought Big Stick was on the run," said Ferdinand.

"Shit, no, he ain't on the run," said Weasel. "He's fucking running shit, man."

Ferdinand sat back and pondered his condition. "Well, what's this got to do with me?" he asked.

"Nothing. I'm talking about *me*, Ferdinand," Weasel responded.

"But why did Big Stick try to kill me?"

"I don't know. Why does that maniac do anything?" Weasel glanced over at Penelope to make sure she wasn't listening and then said under his breath, "Although I did hear that Constant Love was brain screwing you before he lost it. I read what *The Slanted View* had to say. What a joke ... pissed off at the Hedonist's agenda. Shit."

"But, if the tuffies are working with Big Stick, why didn't he kill me?" asked Ferdinand.

Weasel got up from the bed and started pacing back and forth. After a couple of laps, he suddenly stopped and looked up at Ferdinand. "I have no idea," he confessed. "Shit, Ferdinand, I don't know if that's a good sign or a bad sign."

Ferdinand thought for a moment then said, "Why would the tuffies want me alive?"

"Maybe because they didn't want to have to cover up for Big Stick," said Weasel. "You know, they didn't want the attention."

"Cover up?" wondered Ferdinand aloud. "He killed fourteen! What difference would one more make?"

"He didn't kill fourteen," said Weasel. "He didn't kill anybody. Shit, that guy couldn't hit a barn with a fucking hand grenade."

"Well, he hit the Jalapeño," said Ferdinand. "What about the article?"

"Shit, *The Slanted View* just wants sales, Ferdinand. They haven't written an accurate, interesting thing in years. They made all that crap up. I had this guy come up and ask me some questions, and I just said 'ya' and 'no,' shit like that. They write whatever they want. They just like to stir up trouble. And look at that fucking Hedonist, what's his trip?" said Weasel, pointing at the electrovision.

"Then maybe she's not alive," said Ferdinand.

"Who?" asked Weasel.

"Constant Love," said Ferdinand.

Penelope turned and stared at Ferdinand. "Is that all you care about?" she demanded.

Ferdinand was caught off guard. He didn't say anything.

Penelope turned around and hugged Abbot, a flood of tears bursting from her eyes.

Ferdinand turned his attention back to Weasel. Weasel was looking at Penelope and Abbot, as if noticing them for the first time.

Weasel got close to Ferdinand and whispered, "No, she's alive Ferdinand. I went to your place after the shooting to ask you about the crackle but you weren't there. As I was leaving, who walks up but A.J. and no other than Constant Love. I lost A.J. when we ran out of the lounge. He said she gave him a ride back to your hovel, although I'm not sure why. You might want to get home, Ferdinand. There's no telling what A.J. has done to your place by now. He's probably smoked all your crackle and torn the place up looking for more."

"Thanks," mumbled Ferdinand.

Weasel turned and proceeded to leave the room but stopped in the doorway. "You know," he said. "I'm bothered by the fact that Big Stick didn't kill you. You know, not like that ... but it doesn't make sense. Maybe that's it; maybe they just didn't want the attention. The point is, I don't know how far this thing goes up. I don't know where this tuffie gets it. It seemed like a lot, Ferdinand, like much more than you could get from petty criminals. You know, like maybe they manufactured it. Maybe Big Stick *did* lose it over that address by the Hedonist, you know, like to cover up the ultimate connection — to keep it in the streets, at least in his fucked-up mind — or maybe *The Slanted View* just printed it that way. Anyway, if that's the case then you'd better watch it, Ferdinand, because you're the only one who could testify in the Big House that Big Stick lost it over Constant Love, not pressure from the Hedonist and his bureaucratic Slime Rot, thereby implying the connection. On the other hand, he'd kill you for Constant Love anyway."

Ferdinand stared at Weasel. "Weasel," he said, "you're a sick boy."

"Just keep your eyes open, Ferdinand," said Weasel as he walked out.

"Wait!" yelled Ferdinand. "I want to go with you!"

Penelope sprang forward and screamed, "I can't take this!"

Ferdinand replied, "Penelope, I love you. Now, leave me alone."

"Ferdinand ..." began Penelope, but she couldn't finish her sentence. She feigned collapsing and Abbot caught her, his expression grim and earnest.

"You don't know what you're doing, Ferdinand," Abbot pleaded. "The milky harvest of the eclipsed monolith is singing to us!"

Ferdinand blinked his eyes. Weasel was waiting anxiously by the door.

"Let's go," said Ferdinand.

3

THE BURNING

"**M**an With No Name, blow your fucking whistle," stated Altruistic Joe, defiantly. He took a puff of crackle, blew out the venomous fumes, and handed the pipe to the person on his left-hand side.

A.J. was still in Ferdinand's hovel, sitting cross-legged in the middle of the living room floor in a circle with fifteen others. Each person, including A.J., was dressed in a psychedelic burlap jumpsuit and wore a headband that said PMF Angel. The entire group smelled of dirt and rank body odor. They were eating mushy grains with wooden spoons from wooden bowls, and they were planning a terrorist attack on the Quagmire. In the background, tribal drums played syncopated rhythms from the stereo. Bins and sacks of crackle were littered about the hovel.

"The Quagmire must learn to tolerate complacency," said the leader of the circle. "Man's desire to feed off the system is tantamount. We are the children of one another. We are each other's brethren. Smoke crackle with me, people, and plan the coming of the Quagmire's resistance to coin hoarding!"

A.J. pounded his fist on the floor. Each member of the group tapped his or her spoon against their respective wooden bowls.

"Fuck the man!" A.J. shouted.

"You are right to care so much, our new brother," said one of the PMF Angels. "We will be with you in spirit when you lay the bomb to rest in the belly of the Quagmire."

A.J. studied a map of the Quagmire. Various subjects partitioned the Quagmire's buildings: Development of Agreements, Resolution of Disagreements, Mathematics, Sciences, Social Behavior, Botany, Aesthetics, and Athletics. In the center was the Quadrangle. In the center of the Quadrangle was the Coronation Monolith, a memorial to those who lost their lives in the legendary fight against the interlopers of the Outlands. A.J. was to set a bomb atop the Coronation Monolith.

"I have not heard the bird song," said A.J. "When do we land within the cooperation tenements and live as one, collectively?"

The PMF leader spoke. "That time is not yet at hand, oh yearning one. The People's Militia Force is well, collecting coins from the masses, but the evil distribution lords have seen to it that the coin hoarding continues. Oh, may we bask in the mighty collections, their hands in our tills, their tentacles reaching far! But we must *all* be allowed to wash underneath the coin waterfall, my brethren. Heretofore, the Quagmire has preached competitive practices designed to crush the whole of the heart. We must stand together and forge our way so that all may join to become one under our communal sun. Only then may we smoke crackle freely within our celebrated cooperation tenements. As it is my word, A.J., you shall be made Holy Janitor of the Tenements when that time is at hand."

Thoughts of stinky drab work garments, buckets of shit, bright vegetable gardens, and unreserved love flashed through A.J.'s mind. "An endless supply of crackle," A.J. muttered to himself.

"Now then," continued the leader, "we must plan for the coming destruction so the Quagmire learns to respect the collective. Tomorrow the deed shall be done. A.J., you must center yourself. Smoke the illuminant rock with us and plant your psyche firmly in the firmament. We shall make you a pass so you may slip freely within the Quagmire, posing as a legitimate student, eager to learn the competitive ways. You shall remain undetected in your white cloud. And then you shall return to us, having blown certain portions of various edifices to smithereens."

"Yes," agreed A.J., as he ignited a bit of crackle on fire and sucked in its smoke.

"Now let us celebrate the coming of the new age," said the leader.

Someone from the group got up and turned up the tribal music. Various people around the circle sucked from their crackle pipes. The group again began to drum rhythmically against their wooden bowls, chanting laboriously to the beat while fragments of sticky grains spewed from their teeth and splattered the rugs of Ferdinand's hovel.

FERDINAND AND WEASEL sat idly in their railcar on the Corkscrew Rail. To their left and down the rail, a congestion crew dressed in orange baggies was working on the rail, simultaneously wrecking and soldering portions of the track. Below the track, huge pieces of equipment were digging and churning the bedrock, spewing black particles of earth and pollution into the air. The entire sky was a sickly yellow and grey. All cars on the rail were blocked and motionless.

"What the fuck is going on?" asked Ferdinand.

"The Hedonist is building the Lifeline Rail," answered Weasel. "It will connect Barnacle Row with Fern Lane, diagonally, across Rockville. Can you imagine?"

"What the hell for?" said Ferdinand.

Weasel continued, "So that 'the people may know the generosity of the Hedonist,' and 'to stimulate economic recovery within the under-valued portions of the state,' according to the Hedonist."

Ferdinand sighed. "I think I'm going to throw up," he said.

"Don't even think about it, "said Weasel, eyeing Ferdinand carefully.

Ahead of them, the bottleneck seemed to be easing as the cars on their track slowly moved forward, shifting to the left side of the track, and continuing at a moderate speed down the rail. They'd only gone some 200 feet before they were again stopped. Meanwhile, the cars on the opposite side sat parked, waiting their turn.

"This is the most idiotic thing I've ever seen," said Ferdinand. "That asshole! We've got to sit here, wasting our lives, while that brain-dead hedonist.... Fuck!" Ferdinand screamed in disbelief.

"Here," said Weasel, handing Ferdinand a crackle pipe. "Smoke some crackle — it will help the time pass more slowly."

"I don't want the time to pass more slowly, you fucking moron!" Ferdinand retorted.

"Fuck you!" said Weasel. "I offer you some free crackle and all you do is complain. Shit! You little mama's boy! Pussy! Asshole!"

Enraged, Ferdinand shoved Weasel, nearly knocking him out of the car and over the side of the track to his certain death below. Weasel countered by regaining his balance, suddenly pulling out a 9-millimeter semiautomatic handgun from his baggies and shoving it into Ferdinand's bandaged ear.

"Now you listen to me, you little prick," he said. "You mind your little pussy manners while you're in my company or I'll do you right here, you understand?"

Ferdinand, feeling nauseous and on the brink of passing out, summoned all his remaining strength to smash a right uppercut into Weasel's groin. Weasel grunted horribly and fired the gun, missing Ferdinand. Wracked with pain, Weasel fell forward into the seat. Ferdinand seized the opportunity to snatch the gun and jam it awkwardly into Weasel's mouth. Weasel, abruptly recovering from his initial pain, used his arm to wrench the gun from Ferdinand's hand while twisting his head from around the barrel.

The two sat sweating in the railcar, panting for breath. Weasel was holding the gun tightly, pointing it at the floor of the railcar. He took a moment to size up Ferdinand. Finally, he said, "Never mind."

Slowly, the cars moved forward again. Underneath the Corkscrew

Rail, below Ferdinand and Weasel, a group of hapless had gathered. The group was throwing rocks and cans toward the congestion crew working on the rail.

Ferdinand sat up to witness the spectacle. "What's that about?"

"The hapless are pissed off, Ferdinand. This Lifeline Rail is cutting straight through the inner sanctum, where they congregate. The congestion crew is tearing up their makeshift hovels."

The conflict was gaining momentum below them. The hapless were becoming increasingly violent, spurred on by many of the frustrated railcar passengers. The congestion crew appeared to be gathering together a counterattack. Ferdinand noticed that two of the crew members were setting up a rocket launcher.

"Look at this," said Ferdinand, tapping on Weasel's shoulder.

Weasel turned his head. "Oh, fuck," he said.

As the two of them watched, the assembly of the rocket launcher was swiftly completed and one of the orange-baggied crew members stuffed a large warhead into the firing chamber. As the hapless continued their onslaught of rocks, cans, and glass bottles, the front lines of the congestion crew parted in unison and they screamed "Bon-voyage!" as they madly fired the rocket launcher at the hapless below.

The warhead blasted directly into the middle of the hapless congregation, sending fragments of body parts into the air and littering the rail with cauterized flesh. The railcar passengers were horrified. Ahead of them, the congestion crew was celebrating. Crew members were slapping each other on the back and breaking out beers in the sickly, smoke-filled air.

Pissed off by their blatant celebration, Weasel lifted his gun and began to fire wildly at the congestion crew. Other passengers pulled out guns of their own and joined Weasel in the riot. The congestion crew fired back. Sparks and metal once more flew by Ferdinand, who was ducking down within the railcar's front seat.

"Get us the hell out of here, Weasel!" Ferdinand screamed.

"I'm doing the best I can!" Weasel screamed back. He continued to fire short blasts into the congestion crew, quite obviously caught up in the excitement of it all.

"The hell you are," objected Ferdinand. "What are you going to do, kill them all?"

As the melee continued, many of the northbound cars began to surge forward, smashing forcefully against the cars in front of them. As the pressure mounted, the foremost cars were pushed off the track, spiraling to their demise below. The surging mass of cars behind them crammed through the destruction like a jointed, metal snake slithering swiftly to freedom, northward. Weasel plopped back down into the rail-car, next to Ferdinand.

"That's it! I'm buying a gun!" exclaimed Ferdinand.

"Shit! You don't have one?" inquired Weasel, whose tone was an aberrant mixture of amazement and disgust.

"No, Weasel," said Ferdinand. "If I had a gun, I would have shot you in the face already."

"Oh, I see," Weasel said sarcastically.

The car leapt forward along the track, leaving behind the dust and destruction of progress. Neither of them said another word until reaching the Northern Hinterlands Station en route to Ferdinand's hovel. Along the way, Ferdinand thought peacefully about Bonvoyage.

As FERDINAND and Weasel approached the door to Ferdinand's hovel, they could hear the loud bongo rhythms of music inside. Standing next to each other in front of the door, they shared a concerned glance while Ferdinand slowly worked the key.

Inside, the hovel was pandemonium. A.J. was naked and hoisted on the shoulders of a PMF Angel, who was staggering about the front room chanting incoherent gibberish. The remaining PMF Angels were littered about the room. Some had passed out, some were smearing body paint on their faces and chests in a display of tribal symbolism, and others were eating off the floors and counters. The hovel reeked of rotting grains and sour meat. Clouds of crackle whispered through the stale air. Tins, baggies, piles of crackle, and crackle pipes lay indiscriminately about the entire place. Weasel stood with a slight grin on his face while Ferdinand stood in amazement and disbelief before the scene.

Five minutes may have passed before Ferdinand snapped out of his dazed amazement and stormed inside, ranting and raving madly about the room. At the onset of this intrusion, the PMF Angels sprang into action and quickly grappled Ferdinand, pinning him to the floor. Ferdinand was kicking and screaming profanities at A.J., who looked completely dazed, as if he were thinking that Ferdinand had risen from the dead.

Weasel stood back, enjoying the scene. Finally, he pulled out his gun and ordered that Ferdinand be released. They did as he instructed.

Ferdinand sat up, trying to catch his breath. Slowly, he muttered, "A.J., what are you doing?"

A.J. simply stared back at Ferdinand blankly.

A PMF Angel interceded, "Who the hell are you?"

"I live here, asshole," replied Ferdinand.

"Never mind," countered the PMF Angel. "Your hovel has been appropriated by the PMF Angels as it is necessary to the furtherance of our collective cause, of which I am sure you are in full support."

"The hell I am!" Ferdinand yelled. "A.J., tell this asshole to get the fuck out of here, and come to think of it, get the fuck out yourself. What happened to you?"

A.J. finally spoke. "Ferdinand, if you could see the progress we've made since you left ... the plans we've developed. It's a new society, Ferdinand! It's a new tomorrow. Crackle is togetherness, you know?"

Ferdinand asked, "Is this about The Man With No Name?"

"Hell, no!" A.J. yelled. "This is about receiving, not giving."

Ferdinand sat on his floor, not knowing, again, which way was up and which way was down.

Weasel, sensing the opportunity, decided to take control of the situation. Weasel shut off the music and addressed the group. "Okay, assholes, here's what's going to happen. First, you're going to get out. Second, on your way out, you're going to take your bomb there, and leave *my* crackle, to which you've so generously helped yourselves."

"*Your* crackle!" yelped A.J. "How do you figure that?"

"Constant Love didn't give it to you, A.J.," countered Weasel. "She stole it from Big Stick, who stole it from me, who is hiding it here on some pretense. That makes it mine."

"A.J., put some clothes on," said Ferdinand.

A.J. turned around to slip on his psychedelic jumpsuit. He remained silent. The group of PMF Angels started gathering their things (some of them slipping small portions of crackle into their baggies), preparing to leave.

The leading PMF Angel made a concluding remark. "You shall remember us when the Quagmire is brought to its knees. Do not make an enemy of the people, my foolish two, or you shall be squashed by the hands of justice as well."

"Fuck off," replied Weasel.

A.J. turned to Ferdinand. "Ferdinand, I'm glad you're okay. I've got a new life now. I'm a hero of the people ... or soon will be. You'll hear about the Quagmire devastation tomorrow."

"Shut ... up!" yelled the leader.

"Ferdinand, thank you so much for your hospitality," he finished sarcastically. The PMF Angels and A.J. then walked out, slamming the door behind them.

"What was that about?" asked Ferdinand.

"You know, Ferdinand," said Weasel, "you're always asking me that. That, my friend, was the PMF Angels, of which A.J. is now apparently a member. They're a terrorist group that promotes a one-world collective society through astronomical coin collection from everyone else who works. That seems to be where the logic fails. Anyway, according to A.J., it appears that he's going to be initiated by bombing the Quagmire."

"Fuck, I can't take much more of this," said Ferdinand.

"Well, I guess you don't have a choice," laughed Weasel. "Let's see ... I'm going to take my crackle back, but Big Stick will think that you have it as soon as he beats the shit out of Constant Love. I wouldn't say your relationship with Big Stick is improving, Ferdinand. And, since the Quagmire is about to be bombed by a terrorist group that organized and planned the attack in your hovel — a hovel believed to be filled with illegal crackle — I imagine you might be implicated somehow in that as well. Not to mention the fact that if my earlier theory holds true, the tuffies probably won't like you having all that knowledge — or shall we say evidence — of their crackle being stored in your hovel. But don't worry, I'm sure Constant Love is rock solid when it comes to her love and loyalty for you, Ferdinand."

Ferdinand sat on the floor of his wrecked hovel in disbelief. His world was spinning before his eyes. His head ached, his soul wilted.

"Take me with you, Weasel," pleaded Ferdinand.

"I don't think so," said Weasel. "You're dangerous, Ferdinand. Besides, you're much more valuable sitting right here. I'd get some rest if I were you. You're due back at the caramel factory."

Weasel collected the leftover crackle about the room, stuffed it into a large canvas bag he found laying on the floor, and walked out, leaving Ferdinand spinning and desperate. In the resulting silence, Ferdinand could just make out the continuing address from the Headmaster Hedonist coming from the electrovision in the back room.

"In my muddy palms I smear the blood of the hapless, wrought with tears. Oh, Lifeline Rail! [*gong!*] Oh, Lifeline Rail! [*gong!*] Oh, Lifeline Rail! [*gong!*] Clear my nostrils of their bone dust and pave the ivory path which is their umbilical cord to the promised land! [*gong!*]"

An exhausted Ferdinand escaped to sleep in his own bed, where he dreamt he was a cold, clear stream dancing through meadows, twisting and turning along the banks and feeding the neighboring wild flowers lit gold and violet by the hovering sun, which burned in the colors of Constant Love.

4

STICKS AND STONES

The next afternoon, Ferdinand awoke in a daze. His hovel had been gutted and wrecked and his head throbbed. He knew that it was not safe for him to stay there since Big Stick Hun (and who knows who else) might be looking for him. For the same reason, going back to the caramel factory seemed out of the question, at least for the present.

So, Ferdinand called in unable to work and decided on a course of action. He would gather some essentials in a satchel and try to find A.J. at the Quagmire before the bombing could occur. If he could stop A.J., he could stop any implication in the plot by the PMF Angels. He could also ask A.J. about Constant Love.

Ferdinand took a railcar to the Quagmire, which was southeast of the Hinterlands and northwest of Barnacle Row. Once there, he located the Office of Political Affairs on a campus map. By altering his caramel factory identification card to read as Altruistic Joe Kidde, he hoped to gain a copy of A.J.'s Quagmire enlistment card and class schedule. Once he had the schedule, Ferdinand figured he could track A.J. down.

Ferdinand entered the office. Before him was a stainless-steel counter and a long series of windows that read CLOSED. Behind him and opposite the windows were a group of phones with instructions on the wall. Ferdinand read the instructions, which indicated that all incoming students were to obtain an enlistment card via phone operation, segregated alphabetically by last name, over specified hours. Kidde was to have registered the day before between 2 and 7 p.m.

Nevertheless, Ferdinand dialed the enlistment number. "You have reached the Office of Political Affairs," said the voice on the other end of the line. "Please have your enlistment identification number ready. If you have not yet received your enlistment identification number, you may do so by pressing five now."

Ferdinand pressed five.

"Please enter the first four digits of your last name now," said the voice.

Ferdinand pressed the digits corresponding to K-I-D-D and waited for the recorded voice to continue.

"Your request has been denied," said the voice. "The designated enlistment timeframe of the last name that you entered has expired in accordance with OPA policies. Please comply with OPA policy in the future." The line was then immediately disconnected.

Ferdinand hung up the phone and was beginning to leave when an elderly woman with an Office of Political Affairs identification badge walked through the front doors.

"Excuse me, miss," said Ferdinand. "I'd like to —"

"This office does not earmark funds for personal requests, Mr. ..."

"Kidde," finished Ferdinand.

"Kidde, yes. Please direct any questions through the system. Thank you," said the woman as she walked away.

"Well, fuck you up the ass!" screamed Ferdinand after her.

The woman turned violently and then stopped herself. She reached into her satchel and took out a small handgun. She chambered a round, put the gun back into her bag, and retrieved a crackle pipe. She lit the pipe, all the while staring at Ferdinand. She sucked in deeply and blew her crackle stench directly into Ferdinand's face.

"Suck my cock," she said. "And, Mr. Kidde, I think you'd better fix those bandages on your head before I kick your skull in." She walked to the back of the room, efficiently entered her combination into the keypad, opened the door, and disappeared into a maze of offices sealed safely within the OPA building.

Ferdinand shook his head and left the office, grabbing an enlistment schedule on the way out. To his surprise, he discovered that all new students were scheduled for certain introductory classes. He noted that one such class, Social Behavior, had just begun in Room 342.

After winding his way through a series of cement corridors, Ferdinand found the classroom he was looking for. Through the large glass window in the door, he spotted A.J. sitting in the back, feverishly taking notes on the lecture. Ferdinand paused to listen in.

"The cognitive map is a landmark paradigm. What we see is the connection in dimensionality of the isoblast, meaning the single neuron connection, and the multiblast, having more or less to do with emotional states. Our model presupposes everything and thus concludes that our cognitive map is useful in that context. The further study of this will, of course, lead to further study, which, when published, will be taken seriously by others who publish in an attempt to avoid the doing and replace it with the more advanced thinking about that doing. You will understand this to be the Cognitive Map Process. Thus, if tested, remember the paradigms and resulting consequences. The multifunctional effect is its conclusion; we perceive through those relationships, which interreact with everything we perceive, thus verifying and requiring us to question our model. As you can see, this can only produce progress and papers. But most importantly, it helps us organize and make sense of our world. Thank you."

Ferdinand turned violently from where he stood by the door and threw up. A thick, yellow liquid exploded from his mouth and partially sprayed a group of women passing by in the hall. "Sorry," apologized Ferdinand, still choking back the mysterious contents of his stomach.

"You stupid freak!" yelled one of the girls, hurrying to move by him.

At the sound of the commotion in the hall, the students in the classroom stopped listening and turned their attention toward the hallway, including A.J., who recognized Ferdinand immediately. A.J. sprang up from his seat and ran out of the classroom. He whizzed past Ferdinand and headed down the corridor.

Ferdinand stumbled after him. "A.J.! Wait! I just want to talk to you!"

"The infidels shall pay the price of greed!" called A.J. in return. And with a bolt, he escaped the confines of the corridor and ran across the Quadrangle toward the Coronation Monolith. Ferdinand gave chase but was steadily falling behind. Meanwhile, two campus tuffies had exited the corridor and were chasing after Ferdinand.

As Ferdinand made his way through the Quadrangle, he could see A.J. running up a flight of stairs and into an adjacent building. Ferdinand caught the reflection of his pursuers in the front glass of the building as he followed A.J. inside.

Without warning, the front glass of the building blew out. Ferdinand was thrust backward when heavy metal beams from the building's second floor came crashing down in a thunderous landslide of glass and metal all around him. Ferdinand fell violently against the ground and was knocked unconscious.

WHEN FERDINAND AWOKE he was alone, covered by books and rubble. His head felt broken and his mind ached like it never had before. He wondered whether he was truly meant to breathe oxygen or if the air itself was part of the problem. Everything about his consciousness hurt. He uncovered himself and thought about what he should do: perhaps disappear into the inner sanctum with the hapless or turn in Weasel in exchange for a deal with Big Stick and the tuffies.

Rolling over, he buried his head in a book as if it were a pillow. The pages of the book were slick and glossy. Ferdinand removed his nose from the binding and instinctively perused its contents. In the book was a map that illustrated Rockville and the Outlands. All at once, his dreams took life, lighting fire to his mind.

There before him was his world described. Clockwise from the west was Fern Lane; to the north, the Hinterlands; toward the east, the Quagmire, Big House, hemphouse, Barnacle Row, and the Abomination House; then the Southside with its caramel factory, Homestead Morgue, and Jalapeño Lounge; all of which surrounded the inner sanctum (which was being sliced and cut by the Corkscrew Rail even as Ferdinand lay there). To the east, beyond Barnacle Row, were the Outlands, colored in green. Across the Outlands, the word INTER-LOPERS was written in bright red. Beyond the Outlands, set apart by a thick black line, the map was blank and lightly colored blue.

"It's Bonvoyage!" he realized, gazing into the blank, blue space of the map. "It's beautiful!" In his dreamy mind, Ferdinand basked in the healing blue of his fantasy. In the winter, he walked in the ice caves of Bonvoyage, covered in furs; in the summer months, he floated lazily down its streams and through those grassy meadows of which he had dreamt. With him was Constant Love, wholesome and sensual, feeding him roasted fish and seasoned, buttery vegetables.

Although his eyes were open, Ferdinand's mind was very far from the rubble and destruction of the Quagmire. So far, in fact, that he didn't even see or hear the tuffies approaching until his hands were restrained tightly behind his back by a thick piece of hemp.

"Look what we have here," said one of the tuffies. "Altruistic Joe Kidde," he said, after reading Ferdinand's altered caramel factory I.D. card. "Well, it's my lucky day! Mr. Kidde, so nice of you to join us."

Ferdinand promptly returned to his senses and jumped to his feet. Coming to grips with his dark reality, he bent over and started to dry heave, having nothing left in his stomach to throw up.

"There, there," consoled the tuffie. "You've just got a fur ball! Here, let me help you." The tuffie then landed a devastating blow to Ferdinand's gut.

Ferdinand collapsed, writhing in pain on broken metal and glass.

"It's off to the hemphouse for you, you little terrorist! But, don't worry — your PMF buddy is there too! He told us all about you."

With that, the tuffies led Ferdinand away, dragging him over the rubble.

5

THE LABYRINTH

Ferdinand was imprisoned in the hemphouse — a labyrinth of hemp rope cages from which no prisoner had ever escaped. Recorded messages from the Slime Rot agencies were played repeatedly throughout the hemphouse for the stated reason of rehabilitating the prisoners by forcing them to memorize the never-ending volumes of Slime Rot regulations. The volumes were recited to the prisoners section by section:

Section 426b of the Rockville Renal Code states that all city sewer systems shall require flushing not earlier than 15 days nor later than 60 days from plumbing installation. Installation shall be defined to occur on the earlier of the following: (i) application of plumbing cement to the fabrication grooves upon connection of the last piece leading to completion of the applicable project (hereinafter, the 'application date'); (ii) statement by legislative policy, as described in City Procedures Manual (CPM), paragraph 87f; or (iii) when the Application Date is unknown, then upon the repeated use of those sewer systems by city inhabitants producing at least 400 cumulative cubic inches of waste per day, as measured by the standard daily measurements criteria established by other regulation.

Occasionally, prerecorded messages from the Headmaster Hedonist would interrupt the regulatory droning, such as "That's right, people!" and "Eat it up, maggots!"

Ferdinand thought he might kill himself. He had only listened to half an hour of Slime Rot regulations and was, in all seriousness, contemplating hanging himself with the hemphouse ropes. He was certain that hangings were a daily occurrence here and that the jailing materials were not coincidental.

Just as Ferdinand began climbing up the ropes of his cage to further explore doing himself in, he spotted Penelope and Abbot, along with a tuffie, coming down the corridor toward Ferdinand's cage. Ferdinand dropped to the floor and awaited their arrival.

"Hey, *Ferdinand*, here's some friends," said the tuffie. He threw a ball of caramel into the cage and walked away.

Ferdinand snatched the caramel and sunk his teeth into it like a wild animal.

"Oh, Ferdinand!" cried Penelope.

"I could really use your help now, Penelope," Ferdinand said, in between bites.

Abbot, in sandals and white robes, stared silently at Ferdinand. He had his hand on his chin and seemed to be in deep thought.

"Oh, Ferdinand!" wailed Penelope, even louder.

"What?!" screamed Ferdinand. "What?! What do you want? What did I do? What can you do for *me* and what is *he* doing here?" he finished.

"Ferdinand," repeated Penelope. "A.J. told us. He told us everything. About how he found you — naked! — with the PMF Angels and how you became a terrorist, and how you wanted to kill him, and how you threatened someone in the Office of Political Affairs at the Quagmire. Oh, Ferdinand! What's happened to you?! He told us how you took his identity, bombed the Quagmire, and tried to blame everything on him. He almost died trying to stop you! Oh, Ferdinand, how could you?!"

Ferdinand stared blankly at Penelope. He turned to Abbot, whose expression had become grim in disgust at Ferdinand's moral downward spiral. Abbot opened his mouth to say something but then decided otherwise and closed it. He continued to stare and shake his head from side to side.

Ferdinand lost control. He reached through the ropes, making a move to strangle Abbot. Penelope reacted promptly, chopping down hard with her elbows onto Ferdinand's forearms, nearly breaking them in two. Ferdinand yowled in pain and recoiled back into his cage. He was about to explode into a maniacal frenzy when suddenly a release valve in his brain sent him into spasmodic giggles.

Abbot and Penelope held onto each other, concerned. Ferdinand, still giggling, unzipped his pants and began to urinate. He peed through his cage and onto Abbot's sandals and feet. Abbot stared down for a moment before slowly looking back up at Ferdinand.

Quietly, Abbot commented on the situation. "Your urine merely washes away my anger, brother."

Penelope tried to pull Abbot out and away from the steamy stream while Ferdinand laughed even harder.

Moments later, an instigator walked through the corridor doors and up to Ferdinand's cage.

He looked at Abbot and at the puddle of urine on the floor, then at Ferdinand.

"I'm your instigator," he said. "The Big House appoints you an instigator if you can't afford one yourself. I would recommend that you plead out but there's nothing they want. So, we're pretty much fucked," he said matter-of-factly. "They've got at least two witnesses who will testify against you. You'll probably get life in the hemphouse, unless a miracle occurs. On the average, you'll last two years before you kill yourself. The Slime Rot regulations never stop, day or night. I can't stand it in here."

The instigator looked at Penelope and Abbot again. "You two should leave now," he said to them.

Penelope kissed Abbot on the cheek and said, "Let's go."

As they turned to leave, Abbot said, "The Man With No Name will froth the yeast of forgiveness, Ferdinand, and feed you with the rising dough of tomorrow's carbohydrates." With that, they walked down the corridor and out the doors.

"Freaks," said the instigator. "Look," he continued. "I hate to admit it, but that about covers it. It's really just procedural at this point. If you get visitors, try not to say anything. If you want to talk to me, ask the tuffies and they'll get ahold of me. Take care."

The instigator turned and walked out. Ferdinand zipped up his pants and was about to return to the dimensions of his cell when, without warning, Constant Love entered the corridor.

Ferdinand was beside himself. He had just pissed all over the floor; he smelled horribly of sweat and vomit, his bandages were hanging from his beaten and bloodied skull, and he was so tired that he was fading in and out of reality. All the while, Constant Love radiated like an emerald sun. She walked toward him with purpose and heat, like a diesel engine was moving her. Ferdinand was attempting to straighten his bandages and make himself more presentable when she reached his cage.

She was dressed in a tight emerald-green jumpsuit that matched the color of her eyes and complimented her olive skin. The entire hemphouse was electricity personified the moment she walked in the door. Moreover, rather than generating a lurid display of sexual deviance, her presence seemed to command the respect of a queen bee amongst drones who manned their post, ready to die for her.

She stood before Ferdinand and opened a small, black handbag. Lifting a crackle pipe to her lips, she lit the crystalline rock in a single, fluid motion and, almost pouting, sucked in a long, hard puff. Eventually, she exhaled the industrial waste into Ferdinand's gaping mouth.

"Are you my daddy?" she asked, anticipating an affirmative response.

Ferdinand only stood there. His mind sat blank. He felt faint and anxious. He was useless and becoming helplessly aroused.

"Ferdinand," she said. "I've got something for you." She motioned for Ferdinand to come forward.

When he did, she slowly pushed the pipe through his lips. She lit the pipe and he sucked in the familiar gas. It hit him in the temples like an iceberg. The room began to spin as he danced with consciousness, falling backward into his cage.

"Fer-di-nand," she sang. "Fer-diii-naaand."

He was slobbering and jiggling like a Jell-O St. Bernard when Constant Love seemingly fired a piercing beacon of light right between his eyes. The light blasted his fading consciousness back into the hemphouse.

"Ferdinand!"

His eyes opened, big and round, waiting for Constant Love to tell him what to do.

She resumed her sedating tone. "You have something for me, Ferdinand."

He waited, not certain whether she was telling him something or asking him something.

"My crackle, Daddy. I believe you have my crackle."

Ferdinand still just sat there, but was slowly regaining his wits. She waited.

"I don't have it," he said. "But I can get it. Get me out of here and I'll get it." When he heard himself say the words "Get me out of here," it was as if he was in a tunnel. Maybe it was survival instinct, maybe it was the Slime Rot regulations, or maybe it was the crackle and caramel driving him slowly toward madness; maybe it was that he had reached bottom and could now only go up or maybe it was all of the above, but he had made the play.

"Ferdinand," she said again. "Do you know who I sleep with? Remember my man — the one with the biggest gun in town? He can reach you in *here*, Ferdinand."

A crazed Ferdinand shot back, "Bullshit, Love! I know you drove A.J. back to my hovel that night to deposit the crackle where Big Stick couldn't find it. If you wanted to involve Big Stick, you wouldn't be here talking to me!" Ferdinand was shaking but found that he was gaining strength.

"Maybe he sent me first," she countered. "And now he's going to tear you limb from limb."

"Big Stick doesn't strike me as a man with much finesse," said Ferdinand. "Besides, does it look like I've got a lot to lose?"

Constant Love reached for her pipe and treated herself to another puff of crackle. Ferdinand waited and hoped desperately that she wouldn't leave.

"What makes you think I can get you out of here?" she asked.

"Tell Big Stick that I've got the crackle. I won't involve you. Tell him that Weasel Salsa, along with the muscle of the caramel factory unions, is moving in to control the Southside. Tell him I'm their point man — that they used me as a pivot to spring a double switch on Big Stick when Weasel approached him, and that Weasel, who took the crackle, was merely a front for the United Caramel Factory Workers. Tell him he's been played like a cheap bongo drum and if he wants in, he's got to go through me. I know he's got some connection with the tuffies, so you tell him if he wants a piece, he better spring me and I'll see what I can do to cut him in. And just to sweeten the pot, if he wants Weasel, I can deliver him too. You go tell him that." Ferdinand winked at her, then took a big bite of caramel, enjoying the moment.

Constant Love stood there smiling. She seemed so proud and amused with Ferdinand, as if she were watching her own little baby take its first steps. "Why don't you tell him yourself?" she asked.

Ferdinand sat on his haunches, bewildered. Then he heard the doors down the corridor open and saw Big Stick appear before his cage. Constant Love stepped back as Big Stick pulled out a 9-millimeter handgun and fired five times, hitting Ferdinand once in his bad leg.

Ferdinand was writhing in pain when two tuffies opened his cage. Big Stick sauntered into the confinement and grabbed him.

"Let's go, dough boy. Why don't you take me to that crackle of mine," Big Stick seethed into Ferdinand's ear.

Constant Love feigned kisses at Ferdinand while he was being dragged down the corridor.

6

PHANTASMAGORIA

Ferdinand had been thrown into the back seat of Big Stick's car. They were rapidly speeding away from the hemphouse. From the driver's seat, Big Stick commanded, "Tech! Fix his leg! He's bleeding all over the place!"

In the back seat with Ferdinand, a technician was smoking crackle. In a daze, Ferdinand looked at him and hoped he wouldn't amputate his leg or otherwise stick him with dull metal instruments. The technician reached into a black bag on the floor and pulled out gauze, rubbing alcohol, and some dull metal instruments.

Big Stick waited a beat, then said to Ferdinand, "Ferdinand, the technician here isn't very good. In fact, he's a real fuck-up. But if I really cheer him on, he can do a bang-up job. So why don't you tell me where I can find my crackle?"

"Weasel's got it," Ferdinand stammered. "Weasel Salsa took it from me even though I never really had it. I didn't even want it! A.J. — Altruistic Joe Kidde had it! After Constant Love stole it from you, she and A.J. hid it at my place and then Weasel took it — yesterday, I think."

From the front seat, Constant Love shot a look back at the technician. The technician pressed his thumbs hard into Ferdinand's wound. Ferdinand cried out in agony from the pain.

Constant Love explained, "I moved it, Ferdinand — for safekeeping. Please don't attribute such base motivations to my conduct. What have I ever done to you?"

Ferdinand was about to pass out when the technician stopped.

"Okay, dough boy," said Big Stick. "Where do we find Weasel?"

"I don't know where he lives," Ferdinand gasped. He was sucking through his teeth in a struggle for short, hard breaths. "He's probably at work at the caramel factory. Anyway, they'll have his address there."

"You sure the United Caramel Factory Workers are going to be happy to see me?" said Big stick, grinning into the rearview mirror.

Ferdinand said nothing.

"Okay, tech, fix him up. But remember, Ferdinand. If we don't find Weasel *and* my crackle, I'm going to shoot you in the face."

With that, the technician handed Ferdinand the crackle pipe, letting Ferdinand smoke himself into unconsciousness before beginning the work on his leg.

In his stupor, Ferdinand swirled and sank into a damp, grassy hillside. His limbs became winter branches and his fingers became autumn leaves. His hair was moss. He communicated with the birds that nested on his shoulders. They whispered to him. They said, "True, 'tis meaning which brings you here. Tra la la! The light in your eyes is the home of our hearts. Tra la la! Fly, fly, fly. Tra la la. 'Tis true. Tra la la. Our mighty warrior!"

Ferdinand blinked in his dream and his eyelashes threw back tears over the birds' wings and his eyes were bright suns that warmed their backs. The birds grew, exponentially, from the warmth and the tears and became giant, beating creatures that sank Ferdinand deeper and deeper into the grassy hillside from their increasing weight until he ultimately awoke on the floor of the car, his head newly wrapped with bandages, resting on a pile of blankets.

"Butthole! Let's go!" Big Stick called out. "We've got some crackle shopping to do."

Ferdinand sat up. They were in the parking lot of the caramel factory. Big Stick was waiting for him outside of the car with an AK-47 slung around each shoulder, a handgun stuck into the front of his baggies, and a black headband wrapped just above his eyes. Ferdinand got out and walked ahead of Big Stick into the caramel factory and up to the front desk.

"Hey, is that you, Ferdinand?" the desk person inquired while munching on a thick ball of caramel. He looked at Ferdinand, then back at big Stick Hun.

"Yeah, it's me. I've been out sick, you know. You seen Weasel Salsa?"

"No. Why you askin', Ferdinand?"

"Because I am, that's all." Ferdinand replied.

"Well, he ain't here. He's dead, Ferdinand, if you didn't know. I heard about it this morning. Tuffies found him dead not too far from your place up in the Hinterlands. What the fuck happened to you anyway?" he asked.

Ferdinand stood there speechless.

Big Stick walked up to the desk, pointing the handgun into the face behind the counter. He asked, "What do you know about it?"

The desk person responded steadily. "Just what they said on the electrovision — the PMF Angels are claiming responsibility relating to some cause or something. They showed a picture of that leader guy."

Big Stick turned the gun toward Ferdinand. "What's next?" he asked. "This is your dead end, not mine."

Ferdinand stammered back, "A.J., he's with the PMF, the People's Militia Force ... Angels. They're a subversive, coin-collecting terrorist group that —"

Big Stick interrupted. "I don't give a fuck what they are! You've got about five seconds to figure out where I can lay my hands on my crackle or I'm going to break your knees with the tip of my boot and then shoot you in the throat."

The desk person stared from behind the desk at Big Stick.

"Maybe they went back to my place. That's where they were before," Ferdinand said.

"Sounds like *you're* a PMF Angel, Ferdinand. If I didn't know what a little fucking turd you are, I'd think you've had your hand in this the whole time. Come to think of it," Big Stick continued, "I'm going to have myself a look around *here* first."

Big Stick grabbed the keys from behind the front desk and locked the door. "Stay here, Ferdinand," he ordered. Big Stick turned to focus again on the man behind the desk. "If he's not in this room when I get back, I'm going to kill both of you."

Big Stick left the room, exiting to the right between the two swinging doors that led to the floor of the caramel factory.

The man behind the desk scoffed. He picked up a phone and placed a call while Ferdinand waited impatiently in the front room. "The vice president wants to talk to you anyway."

FIVE MINUTES LATER, the vice president arrived, looking upbeat and gregarious.

"Ferdinand? I'm Vice President Johnson. Why don't we sit down?" he suggested, pointing to two chairs.

Ferdinand sat down, then quickly jumped into conversation. "Yes sir, I've been sick and —"

"Yes, yes," Johnson interrupted. "Terrible business. But it's not about that, Ferdinand."

Ferdinand waited.

"Your position has been upgraded, Ferdinand. You see ... or perhaps you haven't heard ... but in any event, there's the compubox now. Really, Ferdinand, it's our collective friend, speeding up processes and efficiencies like the wheel. It *is* a wheel of sorts, I guess — a wheel of progress! The compubox, Ferdinand, is going to change Rockville forever, and we've got to stay up with the times. Anyway, most of the positions here are now expendable, including yours, which will be manned by the compubox. You wouldn't think it could taste, would you? You'd be surprised, Ferdinand! The manpower within each compubox is staggering! Oh, of course, there will be sacrifices and lengthy, expensive, and time-consuming training ... in conjunction with the Quagmire ... but before long, Ferdinand, we'll be upgrading to new systems, each one staggeringly more complex and dependent on compubox technology than the last, requiring enormous investment and downtime, until the whole factory can be run by the ultimate utopian system. That system, Ferdinand, is the human mind stripped of unproductive feeling, awareness, and wisdom. You know what I'm saying?"

Ferdinand sat there with his mouth open, but speechless. He finally managed to ask, "What about everyone's jobs?"

"Oh, don't worry, Ferdinand, we haven't forgotten about that! Most of you, with the exception of you, specifically, Ferdinand, will be working right here. You see, we've been selected for Slime Rot regulation, so most of the *physical* work will now be shifted into *compliance* work. That is, we've got to make sure we comply. So, we've got most of the crew pouring over countless manuals, Ferdinand. It's very important and exciting work. Several are going to work for the Slime Rot agencies themselves. After all, who knows how to regulate our business better than the people who used to run it? You might want to look into that, Ferdinand," Vice President Johnson pointed out. "And, finally, the others are going to work for the congestion crews. They've been beefing up their numbers due to the increasing casualties on the Lifeline Rail. Oh, and I almost forgot — everyone else has been shifted into the Human Resources department."

"What human resources?" Ferdinand asked.

"We also have your severance, Ferdinand," Johnson continued, ignoring Ferdinand's remark. "Now, it's not in coins, as you might have expected. It's in credits. I don't know how long you were down, Ferdinand, but a lot has changed — for the better — since you last bit into a delicious caramel glob here at the factory. The Headmaster himself announced the extinguishment of the coin standard, Ferdinand. We've all gone to credits, which will be responsibly controlled by the Feeding Frenzy Board and tracked by the compubox. That distinguished board,

comprised of anonymous, elite members from wealthy families —
Quagmire educated, of course — will determine how the economy
ebbs and flows, Ferdinand, ebbs and flows. Now, I can't expect you to
understand this all at once, but it allows speculation, Ferdinand. That
great industry of thinkers and know-it-alls, together with the assistance
of the compubox, somehow create and consume value in the free
markets of the industrial age, providing officers and those in control
with healthy, speculative compensation packages. If things get too hot,
Ferdinand, the Feeding Frenzy Board knows what to do. And, if things
get too *cold,* they know what to do. That is, Ferdinand, they tighten and
loosen their hold on those elusive credits. Now, since the FFB and the
Slime Rot agencies work in conjunction, Ferdinand, they know best
how much to collect. The point here, Ferdinand, is that with the new
regulations and cooperative efforts of the FFB and the Slime Rot, your
severance amounts to two credits. That's the equivalent of one coin."

Ferdinand fell to his knees and vomited all over the floor. The vice
president briskly left the room after first instructing the desk person to
clean it up and to assist Ferdinand outside. Ferdinand was still heaving
convulsively when Big Stick came back, dragging Abbot with him, who
had just reported for his regular shift on the factory floor.

Big Stick trotted over to Ferdinand and kicked him in the gut. "Stop
puking!" he commanded, "or I'll kick you again."

Ferdinand doubled over, trying desperately to breath.

Big Stick looked at Abbot and said, "Pick him up and get him in the
car. And make sure none of that puke comes with him. Wipe it off on
those fucking robes of yours if you need to."

Abbot picked up Ferdinand and helped carry him to the car. Big
Stick opened the door, shoving them both in the back with the technician. Big Stick hopped in front with Constant Love, then took off
toward Ferdinand's hovel.

Big Stick started in again. "Your prophet friend back there tells me
that you're really a member of the PMF Angels, Ferdinand, and that A.J.
had nothing to do with this. Since one of you is lying, I've decided to
take both of you with me."

Ferdinand sat silently in the back seat, his body heaved over in a physical display of exhaustion. He was feeling miserable and wretched.

Abbot spoke up. "The vomit hue of my robes only radiates the crusty warmth of the light emanating from the eyes of The Man With No Name."

The technician got a pipe out and took a deep puff of crackle off it. He exhaled slowly and deliberately into Abbot's face, then said, "They say The Man With No Name actually has a name."

"They can't prove that," Abbot shot back.

"Oh, yes they can," countered the technician. "The compubox contains data files on each one of us, and your name has to be in there or you don't get your credits. Since The Man With No Name operates his cause as a metaphysical meeting place, I'm sure he has to file for coin-collecting exemption as a noncompetitive organization. It's like those PMF Angels; they support coin collecting, but not from them. Anyway, I'm sure he's not paying all those coins to the PMF. And in order not to pay, they've got to file. And in order to file, they've got to enter a name. Therefore, The Man With No Name has a name."

"Bullshit!" yelled Abbot. "The Man —" but before he could finish, Big Stick interrupted.

"The two of you are going to shut up immediately. Besides," he continued, "The Man With No Name *is* his name, get it? It's his name, and his name is The Man With No Name."

Constant Love spoke up. "You can't say your name is you have no name."

Big Stick shot Constant Love a look.

They continued to drive north toward the Hinterlands and Ferdinand's hovel. Their route took them through the streets of the inner sanctum, where the congestion crews were busy carving the Lifeline Rail into the heart of Rockville.

"What the hell is this all about, anyway?" asked Ferdinand, sitting up for the first time. Above them, the Corkscrew Rail was packed with railcars jammed into an incomprehensible mess. A line of cars extended for as far as the eye could see, and the hapless were scattered

about the streets like ghosts. Ferdinand hadn't known that there were
so many hapless in existence.

"It's called progress, ass wipe," answered Big Stick.

"Actually," said the technician, "It makes perfect sense. You take that
man there," he said, pointing to a whalelike creature passed out in the
gutter. "That man does not suffer from credit collection. He avoids the
forfeiture of his wages while living the good life."

Constant Love took a puff of crackle and passed the pipe to Big
Stick. Big Stick handed the pipe back to the technician who, in turn,
handed the pipe over to Abbot.

Abbot said, "Thank you." He was about to inhale when he realized
what he was doing. "In fact, *no* thank you, very much."

"What?" asked Ferdinand.

"*No* thank you, very much," Abbot repeated, handing the pipe to
Ferdinand.

"That doesn't make any sense, Abbot."

"Yes, it does, asshole!" Abbot insisted. "It means I'm not thanking
you, a lot."

"Don't call me an asshole, you fucking freak," said Ferdinand.

With that, Abbot shot a left jab into Ferdinand's chest. Ferdinand
countered by punching Abbot in the face. Abbot wrestled his hands
around Ferdinand's neck. The two of them continued until Constant
Love yelled at them to stop.

"Stop it!" She reached into the back seat to separate them. Constant
Love directed the technician to sit between the two of them for the
remainder of the trip.

Meanwhile, Big Stick was becoming increasingly frustrated with
the congestion crews and the hapless. Between the two of them, they
had managed to completely fill the streets with trash and debris.

"Fucking animals," Big Stick muttered before pulling out a semiautomatic handgun and firing indiscriminately into the trash-littered
streets. "We'll get there," he said. "We'll get there if I have to kill
everyone in my path."

During this time, Ferdinand was in the back seat, rocking back and
forth. "It's all upside down," he mumbled.

"What?" asked Constant Love, looking at Ferdinand.

"It's all upside down," he said again, louder.

"What's upside down?" asked Constant Love.

"It's all upside down," he said again, still rocking. "Give me some crackle."

The technician handed the crackle pipe over to Ferdinand. Ferdinand lit the crystalline rock to the melting point, sucking in the smoke like he was swallowing the sun. He held his puff in for a long time. His lungs expanded and soared, burning from the inside out. His eyes rolled madly back into his skull, which bobbled on his shoulders as if connected by a spring.

"He's seen the light!" exclaimed Abbot. "He knows the mind of The Man With No Name!"

Abbot grabbed the pipe and frantically tried to smoke, but the rock currently basting Ferdinand's electric brain had already been vaporized. No one was paying attention to anyone, each lost in their own realities.

Big Stick broke the trancelike state of his passengers, calling out, "We're almost there! Tech, it's your job to keep that human waste bag of a man coherent, do you understand me? If we don't find my crackle because he can't communicate, I'm going to cut out your tongue."

"No problem," the technician responded. "I've got just the thing." With that, the technician took out a syringe and with it, gently pulled some clear liquid from a small glass bottle like a feeding hummingbird.

"Adrenaline," he announced. "It'll fix him right up." The technician reached over to Ferdinand and grabbed his arm. He pushed the syrupy liquid into Ferdinand's vein with the syringe.

Ferdinand immediately shot stiff and straight, his eyed fixed on the ceiling. He began to scream.

"Shut him up!" yelled Constant Love, covering her ears.

The technician hit Ferdinand in the stomach, forcing him over. Ferdinand worked to catch his breath. He resumed his rocking at a much faster pace, back and forth, back and forth, while humming the nearly inaudible mantra of "It's all upside down, it's all upside down."

Ahead of them, Ferdinand's hovel appeared in the distance.

BIG STICK PARKED, got out of the car, went to the rear and opened the trunk. From the trunk, he grabbed two or three hand grenades, a couple of knives, a flack jacket, helmet, goggles, gas mask, brass knuckles, steel-toed boots, two automatic machine guns (slinging one over each shoulder), two hand guns, and two gas cans.

"Let's go," he garbled through the gas mask.

Constant Love looked at Big Stick in disbelief, for the first time it seemed.

Abbot was staring up to the heavens. Ferdinand got out of the car. He marched behind Big Stick like a hired mercenary and the others followed suit.

The group approached Ferdinand's hovel, where two PMF Angels stood guard out front, each one armed with a rifle. The door to the hovel had been removed and the entrance decorated with ivy, like that of a makeshift palace. Beads draped the doorframe with two matching, white clay lions situated on either side.

Big Stick approached the guards and started emptying one of the machine guns in their direction. The clay chipped and broke away; the hovel entrance splintered and snapped. The guards fell down from the explosion of bullets and into their psychedelic burlap baggies where they lay motionless, like heaped laundry.

The PMF Angels responded by firing from the windows of the hovel. Big Stick and the rest of the group dropped to the ground for cover. Big Stick grabbed a hand grenade from his jacket and was about to pull the pin when he heard a voice from inside the hovel.

"Big Stick! Stop! We've come together for a new tomorrow! The tuffies, the Headmaster Hedonist, all of us! The PMF Angels and the Hedonist support the new tomorrow — the cooperation tenements. We've come together to move things forward! Listen to your radio!"

"Fuck you and die!" yelled Big Stick. He ripped off his gas mask and emptied the other machine gun in the direction of the hovel before dropping to the ground for cover.

"Big Stick!" the voice yelled again. "You can have the crackle. It's yours! It's ours! It belongs to the cooperation tenements, but you can exchange it — for credits. You've already been given the credits. Listen to your radio."

Constant Love had already returned to the car and was listening to the radio. Big Stick glanced back and took note of her nodding her head affirmatively. He went back to the car and sat down with her. On the radio, the Hedonist was giving an address, which continued in progress:

"The Lifeline Rail, it fills me like a balloon on my birthday. Oh, people! This new day dawning has come like a newborn baby. I've been reborn with it and, together, our panel members, whom you see before you, have tied the ribbons of cooperation: the tuffies, the Feeding Frenzy Board, the Slime Rot, the Malevolent Seven, the Quagmire, the PMF and their Angels and, last but not least, The Man With No Name. All are suckling at my nipple, our collective mother's milk."

Big Stick sat still, expressionless. The violent garb which had empowered him only minutes ago now seemed to hang on him like old skin. He gestured for Constant Love to get up. Together, the two of them got out of the car and walked into the hovel with the technician. Abbot and Ferdinand followed them.

Inside, the hovel had been made into a psychedelic commune. PMF Angels were gathered in groups, smoking crackle and softly playing instruments. They were watching the Hedonist's address on the electro-vision. Behind the E.V., crackle was stacked against the wall in pouches and tins.

"I want to know what happened to the crackle," said Big Stick.

A PMF Angel walked up to Big Stick and asked, "What do you mean?" It was the same voice that had been yelling at them while they were outside.

Big Stick replied. "I mean, how did it get here? Where's A.J.?"

"I'm A.J.," answered A.J. He was sitting with a group on the floor, smoking crackle. He looked up at Big Stick.

"He's going to have to die," said Big Stick. "I'll look into whatever deal's been made in just a minute, but first somebody has to pay for ripping me off, no matter what."

A.J. turned white and started to chatter madly. "I didn't steal it! Constant Love brought it here! She said you were … unstable. She said she needed to keep it where you couldn't get your hands on it for awhile. She told me not to tell you, not to tell anyone. It belongs to the people now."

"Fuck you," said Big Stick. "You think the people are going to keep me from fucking killing you?" Big Stick looked at Constant Love and struck her swiftly across the face with the back of his hand. "Unstable?!? You fucking whore. Trying to rip me off with these little fucking turds … A.J. and Ferdinand? You're all going to die!"

Big Stick pulled out a handgun. A PMF Angel grabbed his arm. "No, we need them," he said.

"Fuck you," shot back Big Stick.

"Look, you don't understand. The rebirth needs death to fertilize the new stalks."

Big Stick stared at the PMF Angel and then kicked A.J. in the gut, sending him spiraling in agony on the floor. He grabbed Constant Love by the arm and Ferdinand by the back of the neck, then threw them into a storage room in the back of Ferdinand's hovel, locking the door.

"You've got about three minutes," Big Stick said. Then he turned his attention to the address on the electrovision.

THE STORAGE ROOM was gutted save for an electrovision on the cold, cement floor, which was blaring the Headmaster's broadcast.

Ferdinand and Constant Love sat motionless on the floor, watching the address. The screen showed a long, arching black table. Present at the table, as indicated by nameplates, were panel members from the Feeding Frenzy Board, the Slime Rot, the Malevolent Seven, tuffie representatives, the Quagmire, the PMF, and The Man With No Name. There was also a nameplate for PMF Angels, with the corresponding seat left blank.

Each panel member was dressed much like an executioner, complete with hood. All wore long, black robes.

Hanging above the panel was the Headmaster Hedonist. The Hedonist appeared to be levitating, although one could faintly make out the lines of some sort of cable hoisting him above the others. The Hedonist was completely naked, save for an extra large pair of diapers. He loomed over the panel, upside down.

"It's upside down," muttered Ferdinand.

The address continued.

"Rebirth. Let me begin. The technicians have been slotted for Slime Rot regulation so as to measure and systematize the doling out of credited benefits and to ensure that the technicians are wiped clean of their thirst for credits, which shall now flow through us. A little here, a little there."

The Hedonist pinched each side of his own diapered bottom.

"Simplicity becomes complexity. The Quagmire must be multiplied. A society of thinkers must control, within the cooperation tenements.

Simplicity becomes complexity. We must redouble our credit collection efforts. The PMF Angels have lent their hands to take from our collective tills. They have foretold of the new credit bathing for us all. Simplicity becomes complexity."

Ferdinand noticed a stash of crackle behind the E.V., pulled a pipe from his baggies, loaded the pipe with a rock, and smoked.

"We must accommodate the lazy and the slouches. We must allow their tongues to lap at our collective cup and feed from that dirty bath water. Simplicity becomes complexity. We must accommodate everything. Individuality will not be tolerated, unless regulated. Permits shall ensure the proper compliance with regulation."

Ferdinand smoked another rock.

"We must allow ourselves to focus on the trivial, so as to miss the obvious, to collect credits for those monarchies we do not know and that arbitrarily rule us, and are appointed, and untouchable, and unreachable by any means save breaking down the very doors we have worked so hard to erect against change. Now is the time for change ... the time to reinforce that hoarding urge that made Rockville so vibrant and industrious and the greatest producer of caramel ever known! Simplicity becomes complexity."

Ferdinand sparked the pipe again and exhaled into a crackle haze.

"Trivial songs and causes about celebrities must distract us so that we may decorate our lives with the fantasy of other people's lives. We, the panel, shall intrude into everything that is touched, tasted, bought, sold, and foretold. We shall do the foretelling. Simplicity becomes complexity. We shall give each other countless awards and allow you to view us through the magic of electrovision."

Ferdinand smoked some more.

"Your opportunity and success shall be proportionate to your obligations to the panel, which shall, through the PMF and the FFB, govern the ebb and flow of your role and credits within the cooperation tenements. Simplicity becomes complexity. You shall be devoted to The Man With No Name, who, because of his noncompetitive status, within which we glorify, we must now refer to as 'X' so as to place a name within the compubox data files. Simplicity becomes complexity."

Ferdinand was smoking increasing amounts of crackle, fiendishly puffing on the pipe. Constant Love sat motionless, staring in silence at the E.V.

"We must live in fear of the unknown. For only through fear can we know control ... and it is through control that we may all come together. Simplicity becomes complexity. We must rely on the majority, although anesthetized by electrovision, we can have confidence in the knowledge that collective rethinking and unified revolution will be achieved, thereby preserving that ageless compromise within nonexistent lines of forgotten equity, left residing on the important-looking Parchment and kept under glass, so as to twinkle in the winking gleam of our feeding officials. Simplicity becomes complexity."

Ferdinand lit another rock.

"We must look the other way when credits flow from nasty habits, for the interlopers of the Outlands are only a step away. It is this foreign threat and necessary credit allocation that justifies our arbitrary selection of legality ... and death. Simplicity becomes complexity. Our historical assassinations shall become the fodder for entertainment, so that, in the comfort of our regulated viewing and snacks, we may enjoy the drama of government without having to know its dimensions. We must shield you from our doings since the electorate has implicitly entrusted its thinking, choice, and authority to us."

Ferdinand's eyes glazed and his heart pounded.

"Yet we shall provide you with a mechanism for choosing by counting yays and nays. Simplicity becomes complexity. And, yet again, we shall shield even ourselves from ourselves by making our leaders accountable to nonelected independent councils, appointed by those leaders, who shall remove those guilty feelings associated with arbitrary and unprecedented raises in income for our public leaders. Simplicity becomes complexity."

Ferdinand was sweating profusely and smoking, and smoking, and smoking the crackle.

"To preserve the cooperation tenements, we shall allow influence through credit contributions, in addition to thick, meaty meals filled with brown gravy and red leather. Credit collection shall be rampant within multitiered government and upon the occasion of any and every exchange. The cooperation tenements shall be aligned with square plots of identical, family-unit dwellings, all under the guilt-leveraged tenants of The Man With No Name. We shall stew in our own waste with thick, mucous air that suffocates those species that are different from us, thereby preserving a toxic paradise for future generations. The new competition shall take place on the sports field wherein we may celebrate the fantasy and identification of challenge through colors and slogans. And the compubox shall be paramount. Simplicity becomes complexity."

With that, Constant Love took the pipe from Ferdinand and proceeded to smoke.

"For what is fault? Fault is judgment and judgment requires division. Fault has no place in the cooperation tenements of the new age where the reliance on Slime Rot feeds that gaping mouth which regurgitates its bureaucratic stew from which we slop with such hungry complacency. All rights shall be a privilege, and the Slime Rot shall regulate privilege with an unrelenting, self-preserving hand of boredom and senseless rulemaking. Whining shall produce legislation. Simplicity becomes complexity."

Constant Love refilled the bowl and smoked again, then passed it back to Ferdinand.

"The result will be specialization in the production of, and furious competition for, an unneeded volume and variety of consumer products, while the world's resources are consumed by the trivial. To stabilize that consumption, we shall burn the food ... for credits ... and transfer those credits to the hapless ... for food. Simplicity becomes complexity. That great Parchment, which lies under glass, shall ensure that as sure as I am levitating upside down, the rights of the degenerate and criminal shall preclude effective minor penalties while preserving the ultimate penalty within a society that does not judge. Simplicity becomes complexity. Let's not forget the Lifeline Rail and its progress. It shall provide the deliverance through our traffic jams and overcrowding, connecting each of us with —"

Ferdinand filled up the pipe with the remaining rock and fired the solid into gas, which he breathed in furiously.

"— the land of opportunity. Bonvoyage!"

And that was it. Ferdinand snapped. In his sweaty, electric mind, he snapped. He hungered for anything tangible. He could taste the experience thick on his tongue. And in his daze, that which became tangible were the four basic elements that he perceived as earth, wind, fire, and water. Each of these sent him into delusions: the first, back to his dream, as the tree of life; the second, the cleansing blast of wind from beyond the Outlands, healing his body and mind and the streets of the inner sanctum; third, the burning heat of white light, cleansing his soul and cauterizing his wounded body; and fourth, drinking the water from his winding stream, which he once was so thirsty for and now longed for again.

Upon rising from the depths of his visions, Ferdinand grabbed Constant Love by the shoulders and drove her to the cement floor. His eyes were wet and his heart pounded.

He kissed her. He kissed her with the thirst of craving and his kisses went deep and were felt in places within her soul that either she had never known or she had kept closed for too long.

He kissed her mouth. He kissed her neck. He bore down upon her, balancing between the edge of pleasure and pain, of delight and fear. The land where she was taken was a new experience, and it swirled about her.

His hands removed her emerald green gown, revealing her soft, olive skin. Her nipples were dark, and he sucked on each one in turn. Below, he entered her, thick and driving, again and again. He picked her up and fucked her. He turned her around and fucked her. He made love to her with the sweetness that his heart yearned for and that he could only find through a female's touch. Her body was his alter and he prayed upon its gentle message that all would be okay, and that he would be whole again.

When he exploded inside her, she became his savior and guide. And he became her future.

SHE STROKED his hair as he lay beside her. They said nothing. And yet, their thoughts drifted to the knowledge that they might both soon be killed.

"We have to get out of here, Ferdinand," she said. He looked around the room. The door was locked. The walls were wooden, affixed to the cement foundation.

"I'll break out," Ferdinand said.

"What do you mean?" asked Constant Love. "We can't go out there, he'll kill us. Plus, he'll know! He'll take one look at me and he'll know."

"Not that way," said Ferdinand.

Constant Love looked around the room. She saw no way out.

Ferdinand stood up and helped Constant Love get dressed. Outside he could hear the PMF Angels and Big Stick talking amongst themselves. The address was over and Ferdinand knew that he had little time. Ferdinand pushed Constant Love behind him with her back to the locked door.

Pointing at a wooden wall, Ferdinand said, "That way."

"What are you talking about, Ferdinand?" she asked. "That's a wall! You're going to break through the wall?"

"Yes," was all he said.

"But they'll hear you," she protested. "We'll never get out in time."

"I only need two tries," he said.

Ferdinand looked into Constant Love's eyes. His eyes didn't look heroic or scared, but rather they looked like they knew something that she didn't, and it gave her confidence.

"Stand back," he said. Ferdinand took a deep breath, crouched down with his back foot leveraged against the door, and threw himself against the wall like a human cannonball. The impact splintered the wall and shook the house. Ferdinand staggered back and crouched again. He looked at Constant Love, took two deep breaths, and then threw himself against the wall again, this time breaking part of the way through the barrier and cutting his right forearm on the splintered wood. Behind them, they could hear Big Stick working the keys in the lock of the door.

Ferdinand staggered back once more, out of breath, and grabbed

Constant Love by the hand. He pressed against the wall with his back foot against the door just before he heard the turn of the lock.

At the precise moment that Big Stick slammed the door open, Ferdinand sprang forward.

The combined inertia launched both Ferdinand and Constant Love out and against the splintered wood with exponential force.

Big Stick raised his gun to fire just as the wood gave way. He fired three times, missing high, as Ferdinand and Constant Love fell through the wall and down a steep hill behind the hovel to the ground below.

Upon landing, Ferdinand was rendered unconscious. He fell into a dream, where he sat at the counter of a café. A waitress walked up in

red, white, and blue baggies and a tiny, pointed hat covered with stars. She asked to take his order.

"How's the corned beef sandwich?" asked Ferdinand.

"The best and only one in Rockville," said the waitress. Everyone gets a serving; it's all you can eat."

"I'll have the sandwich," said Ferdinand.

"Would you like a beer with that?"

"What do you think?" Ferdinand asked rhetorically.

The waitress returned with his sandwich. Rye bread provided the foundation for thin slices of stacked corned beef. A delicious dill pickle and a cold beer completed the meal. Ferdinand ate pleasantly and was satisfied. He asked the waitress how much he owed her for the meal.

"We know who you are," said the waitress. "It's all in the compubox. We've checked your credits and we've priced the meal. Our café is in synchronicity with those that manufacture the meal; we share information. It's all quite ... understood."

"How much is it?" Ferdinand asked again.

"It's one-half of all of your credits until you die, and then it's one-half of all your credits you have left *after* you die."

The waitress pulled out a gun and stuck it in Ferdinand's face. "Bonvoyage, mother fucker!" she exclaimed, and pulled the trigger. When the gun fired, Ferdinand woke up.

7

TEDIOUS LIES

Constant Love pulled Ferdinand down the hill and into a dry creek bed. There she maneuvered him behind some large boulders for cover. Ferdinand was on his back with Constant Love hovering over him. Above them, Big Stick Hun was standing in the broken wall of Ferdinand's hovel, firing shots in their general direction. They didn't know if he could see them or not.

"We need to leave, Ferdinand," she said.

"I know," he mumbled. "We're going to Bonvoyage. It's beyond Barnacle Row and the Outlands. It's beautiful. I've seen it. We can get away from all this, just you and me."

Constant Love simply stared at him, wondering what he was talking about.

As they scanned the area for a safe route of escape, they spotted Big Stick's car speeding into view. The car screeched to a stop where the creek bed ended and the road began. They could see A.J. and Abbot in the car. From the driver's seat, A.J. honked the horn, signaling for them to come get in the car with them.

Constant Love and Ferdinand shared a look and then broke for the car. Big Stick continued to fire down the hill as the two made their way to the car and jumped in the back. The four of them sped away.

In between short, gulping breaths, Ferdinand asked, "How did you guys get away?"

"A.J., who was driving, explained the situation. "When everyone rushed into the back room to see what was going on, Abbot and I headed out the front door and took Big Stick's car."

"Why you, Abbot?" asked Ferdinand.

Abbot turned from staring out the passenger side window to the back seat to face Ferdinand. "I don't know," he said. "It just seems like nothing matters anymore."

"Why?" asked Ferdinand.

"The Man With No Name has a name," he said simply.

"You mean 'X'?" asked Constant Love.

"Yeah, X!" returned Abbot. "X, X, X, X, X! What's that about? X? Now he's got a name, like all the rest! Hello, Mr. X. How are you today? Can I get you some water, Mr. X?"

"Don't you think you're overreacting?" said Ferdinand. "I mean, what's the difference between X and The Man With No Name? Both signify an anonymous person; neither includes any specific informa- tion indicating —"

"The hell it doesn't," interrupted Abbot. "X is like any other name. It's a sound — a guttural sound referring to an individual. The Man With No Name, in contrast, is a specific recognition and representation that the man, whoever he really is, in fact, has no name. It's very spiritual."

Ferdinand stared at Abbot and then looked at Constant Love.

"Okay," he said finally. "Well, it's good to have you along, Abbot. A.J., take us to Bonvoyage!" Ferdinand ordered happily.

"Where?" asked A.J.

"Bonvoyage. It's beyond the Outlands. It's where we're all going. It's a beautiful place, trust me. Besides, you'll all die if you stay here."

They all remained silent until A.J. interrupted the solemn mood by noting that they would soon be caught if they continued along in Big Stick's car.

"I've got an idea," A.J. said. "The PMF procured a hovel rover for the people. I stole it myself. It's huge! There's a couch and a bathroom, all sorts of shit. It was made by a group of congestion crew workers on special assignment. It's a car for the people. They call it the Parchment Mobile because the entire living craft stands for all our rights enumerated in that grand Parchment — which, by extension, truly becomes a living document. It's psychedelic; you can't miss it!"

"I'm not sure that's the perfect getaway car," said Ferdinand.

"No, it will be great," said A.J. "I was the one in charge of it — that, and putting up the barbed wire around the cooperation tenements. When you're not on the inside, you're on the outside, know what I mean?" A.J. turned and winked at Constant Love, who nodded politely.

"Anyway, they're not expecting it for another two weeks. Since the PMF doesn't know that it's done, they won't be looking for it. And, since every other official knows the PMF was on the panel, we'll get the utmost respect on the highways and byways through the inner sanctum to Bunnyville," he finished.

"That's Bonvoyage," Ferdinand corrected.

"Right," said A.J.

"Anyway, it's all the way downtown. I mean, it's really in the innermost part of the inner sanctum. We'll be in it, people, deep in it! Ever been that deep, Love?" A.J. asked.

"Uh, no. Not that deep," replied Constant Love. "This should be quite an experience."

"Damn right!" said A.J. "I have a whole theory about experience in general, you know."

"Save it for the ride in the Parchment Mobile, A.J." said Ferdinand.

"Okay," agreed A.J.

A.J. drove further and further into the inner sanctum. The further they ventured, the more the scenery changed.

"This is unbelievable," said Ferdinand.

"I know," said A.J. "Can you believe it? I mean, whoa! Look at that."

Outside their windows, the streets had changed dramatically. The steel girders supporting the Corkscrew Rail were smeared with graffiti. Writings like "fuck" and other creative expressions of social unrest painted the landscape. Beneath the graffiti, one could barely ascertain the original grey cement and steel. The street was littered with parking tickets. Each of the cars broken down on the side of the road (and there were many of them) had tickets stuffed under the wipers and crammed in the windows.

"Those are parking tickets," A.J. commented. "Those broken down fuckers impede the ability of the roller machines to clean some of the dirt off that pavement there — underneath the trash. I even got one on the Parchment Mobile. I took it out for a test drive and stopped to buy a gaming sheet. I parked in front of one of those liquor and gun stores for about ten minutes and when I came back, there it was."

As their journey progressed, the streets were increasingly more littered with trash and paper.

"Look at that shit," said A.J. "What you've got there is real opportunity. See the streets?

See that stuff, those binders, all the paperwork? That's what you call Gaming Central, the ultimate gaming sheets. Talk about opportunity! That's why the Headmaster is maintaining his popularity despite all this crazy shit. Look at it, the streets are littered with it. I bought one of those smaller gaming sheets and lost. But those bigger ones, shit! You'll never figure that stuff out. You've got the stickers on the front and all those fucking rules on the back, plus paragraph upon paragraph of addenda stuck to exhibits. For example, Paragraph A means this, but part of that is excepted in Paragraph B. You know?

"See there? The instigators are going crazy. The instigators opened up all these shops in the inner sanctum. The instigators process all the gaming sheets for the hapless. The instigators take about fifty percent if one of the hapless wins. That way, the instigators can enter countless times! Plus, the hapless couldn't enter without the instigators. It's like life forms in a symbiotic relationship within the inner sanctum."

Ferdinand and Constant Love stared at each other.

"A.J., give me some crackle," said Ferdinand.

"Sure enough. No problem, boss," said A.J.

Ferdinand sparked the rock and took a deep puff, handing the pipe to Constant Love. After Constant Love, Abbot took a puff and then set the pipe down.

"The instigators do more than that though," A.J. continued.

"They've started the Lifeline Planning Services Program. That's because ... You know, how everyone's so fucking busy? You know, like we all spend all this fucking time just organizing how the fuck we're going to do all this shit in such a small fucking amount of time?"

A.J. took a hit of crackle and broke out three caramel balls, which he handed to Ferdinand, Constant Love, and Abbot. Then he continued his monologue. "Well, the instigators have started capitalizing on *that* fucking problem. It's like this: Let's say you've got to register your car in the morning, do laundry, call some friends, and then, say, buy something, like a wrench. In order to register your car, you've got to drive it over to the fucking place, right? Well, then you're driving unregistered, or close to that, while you're going over there! Then when you get there, after fighting traffic or after you had to take that fucked-up Corkscrew Rail, there's a fucking line! Come to think of it ... many fucking lines, all fucked up and coming out the fucking door and shit. Well, after that you're probably hungry, so you've got to fight your way and pay double the price for a caramel ball.

"Then what? Laundry, was it? Right. So you go home and then get your laundry and then buy soap and wash it and then dry it and then fold it, right? And then you've got to call people, but other people have already called you, right? So, there are more calls now. And then you've still got to buy that wrench. You don't even know where to get it! Anyway, by the time you finish those few things, your entire fucking day is over. Add up all the days and then you die. What kind of a life is that?"

"A.J.!" Ferdinand yelled. "Summarize this idea. Summarize it. Take it as a whole and then process it analytically in your mind so as to provide us with a more abbreviated version, will you?"

A.J. turned to look at Ferdinand. "Oh, yeah. No problem. So, the instigators do it differently. In order to allow others to live without spending all of their time simply complying with vague rules and regulations at every level of experience, the instigators provide you with this incredibly detailed level of analysis. It's like a flowchart, with least-squares deviations of lineation. The result is, you do everything in the most efficient manner if you follow the chart. It's like, let's say you've got some caramel. Well, if you're in your car and let's say you're going to eat it, and one side of the caramel is, let's say, more stale than the other, then the instigators would tell you to eat the side that's a little more stale because that's the side that would get even more stale sooner, especially if it's turned toward the open window of your car."

"A.J.," Ferdinand yelled some more. "Shut up! Just shut up!"

"Fuck you, man," said A.J. "You've got to know this shit. You've got to know what's going on."

They continued to drive deeper and deeper into the inner sanctum. As they continued, more and more trash and flyers and tickets and gaming sheets littered the streets, until the car was crunching over the road and meandering from side to side in an attempt to maintain its high rate of speed.

"And those flyers there — the ones that say 'Fair Share.' See those? That's about the new establishment, man: the Cooperation Tomorrow and the tenements. The officials are finally getting their fair share, and everyone's got to pay their fair share, man. That's how it's got to be or we'll all go into the streets. Look!"

Ferdinand, Constant Love, and even Abbot turned to look. Outside the vehicle, in front of them, the streets were lined with red banners that read "Bonvoyage!"

"What's that about?" asked A.J. "Hey, Ferdinand, isn't that the name of your place? Bonvoyage?"

"That's it," confirmed Ferdinand. "Exactly."

As they continued, the streets became increasingly congested. They were forced to stop every few feet on account of cross traffic and debris.

"Don't worry. We're almost there," said A.J. "It's just around the corner."

Sure enough, within five minutes they were pulling up to a large, windowless cement building. In the parking lot, secure behind a barbed-wire fence was the Parchment Mobile, in psychedelic colors, as promised.

"Wait here while I get the Parchment Mobile," said A.J., retrieving the keys from his baggies. The three of them sat in the car and waited for A.J. to return. Within minutes, he was backing out the oversized craft into the street. The three quickly transferred from the car to the vessel, climbing aboard with A.J.

"Wow!" exclaimed Ferdinand. "A.J., this is amazing!"

"Yeah, I know," said A.J. "Too much, huh?"

Constant Love was poking into cabinets, pulling out the couch, rummaging through drawers. She walked into the bedroom and then into the communication room and then into the Enumerated Rights room. The many passageways, corridors, and rooms left one senseless for direction, lacking a full grasp of the craft's meaning.

"Holy shit," said Ferdinand. "Hey, A.J.," he yelled. "What's this in the back of the Enumerated Rights room?"

"That's the electric chair and the G.R. Board," said A.J. "The electric chair depicts our ultimate penalty. It's in the Parchment somewhere. I mean, shit, there are people out there chopping other people to bits. We can't have that, man."

"What's the G.R. Board?" inquired Ferdinand.

"That's the slang, you know — for good riddance. You know — babies. Bonanza's out of control! There's not enough space in the tenements as it is, and there's only so many credits. There's not an unending supply of credits, you know. The Feeding Frenzy Board keeps it under tight watch. But, think about it man. It's in the Parchment somewhere that the Headmaster Hedonist, and even the Malevolent Seven, can't fuck with our freedoms, including the freedom to choose —"

Ferdinand interrupted. "What's on the other side, on the wall?"

"That's the Slime Rot. You know, that spells out all the ways in which Slime Rot makes our freedom a more meaningful experience. Think about it. If they let you choose to do all the stuff you would do if they didn't say you couldn't do it, you'd end up doing it *for sure*. You'd probably get fat or relaxed or both and then develop other problems. The Malevolent Seven set them up — the Slime Rot, that is. Think about it. It's in the Parchment. Any exchange, or nonexchange, is within the jurisdiction of the Malevolent Seven — and any other Slime Rot they churn up by extension. Besides, the more important stuff's up here."

Ferdinand and Constant Love, with Abbot following, walked up to the front of the vehicle. On the wall were the Ten Golden Paragraphs.

"There it is," said Ferdinand. "Freedom of religion, press, speech, assembly, and petition."

"That's right," said A.J. For example, The Man With —I mean, X — is a credit taker, not a credit maker. And that communication room back there, it's complete with censorship controls for the kids."

Ferdinand stared out the window of the vehicle. Outside, the streets were buried in a stewing mix of a diseased population and grime.

"It doesn't matter if half the kids are being abused or burnt, or smoking crackle or eating too much fucking caramel, man. If they heard *fuck, pud, dick, hump, tits, vulva, schlong, balls,* or *suck* over the compubox or on the electrovision screen, or heard some sad story about someone doing something that isn't Parchment worthy, it's cut out, man. That's just how it's got to be. Fuck, I mean we'd be a bunch of fucking animals if we heard that shit.

"Evolution must continue. That's also why we can assemble, to stand up for our rights, but if we really mean it, they shut you down because you're only hurting yourself. There's got to be order, you know? Besides, yays, nays, that's the way."

"And guns, too?" asked Ferdinand.

"Yeah, the second paragraph there." said A.J. "Man, think about it. It's unfair to the other guy if only *you* get to have a gun. We've got so many fucking guns in this car," A.J. laughed. "But seriously, where do you draw the line? Ultimately, if you want the right to kill someone else using a gun, they've got to have the right to kill you with their gun. Otherwise, it's not a fair fight. That's why the congestion crews are armed. The hapless are armed, too. But if you hoard too many guns, they take that shit down with more powerful guns of their own — to teach you a lesson about gun hoarding."

"And the fourth paragraph, what's that about?" asked Ferdinand.

"That means those biased tuffie mother fuckers can't search this psychedelic bad boy for all those fucking guns, man, unless we shoot their sorry ass first."

"Right on," said Ferdinand.

"Then there's the ninth and tenth ones. Those mean that despite the Headmaster's plan to the contrary, Rockville is (at least theoretically, or at least technically) a dual power system. Like the Hinterlands, they get credits, too. The subdivisions all need to be funded in order to fight the larger credit-funded, central policy-making constituency. Otherwise, the central one will eat the smaller one.

"Besides that, the people have *other* rights, which they don't bother to list. Some think that by implication they've listed them by regulating them through the Slime Rot. You know?"

"It doesn't make any sense," said Ferdinand. "All the streets are crossing each other. Didn't they even think about this at all?"

A.J. steered the big vehicle to the left and right, chugging to a stop and start, as if attempting to miss a series of land mines on the road.

Suddenly, from the back of the vehicle, Constant Love yelled, "Hey! Get in here!"

Ferdinand and Abbot scurried into the communication room where Constant Love was watching the electrovision screen, which was part of the compubox communication room control board.

"What is it?" A.J. yelled from the front.

Ferdinand, Abbot, and Constant Love found themselves staring at the living image of Ferdinand appearing on a talk show.

"Now you look like Ferdinand, but you're not really him, isn't that right?" the talk show host pointed out.

"That's correct," said the Ferdinand look-alike. "But I feel that, given my looks, I know his mind."

"Yes, we can see that," said the host. "So, what kind of a criminal mind are we talking about here?"

"Well, it sounds like a simple point, but it's a critical issue which I think goes to the root of his sick mind and, more importantly, sets up the fall of the cooperation tenemants — which is his will. Actually, the will of his entire gang."

The screen pictured successive photographs of Ferdinand, Constant Love, A.J., and Abbot.

"Holy shit," exclaimed Ferdinand.

The look-alike continued.

"You see, what I hold here is an insurance bill which Ferdinand has failed to pay on time. If he had paid it in a timely manner, he would not have been assessed a late-payment penalty fee of one credit. Now he is simply refusing to pay. The ultimate responsibility is simple.

"As we all know, certain regions of Rockville have been designated as 'safe harbors' for use by technicians. If a technician or service falls outside of the plan, as described in this very detailed, 1400-page brief synopsis of the benefits package, then it is the patient's responsibility to pay the remaining balance; that is, 100 percent. Point in fact, the burden of proof falls on the patient because, you see, the patient is the only one misinformed and, therefore, if able to properly and successfully plead his or her case, repeatedly, then the simple ability to traverse through the maze of recordings, hyperbole, and double talk, not to mention the mind-numbingly stubborn personnel struggling to be advanced into the PMF Credits Denial and Collections Bureau, would have to mean that the patient was both right and had the amazing intestinal fortitude to convey that fact successfully. Ferdinand has done neither. He's essentially out there, right now, as an uninsured debtor. Simplicity becomes complexity via tyranny of the bureaucracy."

Ferdinand began to dry heave. While the rest stared at the screen in disbelief, the E.V. program was suddenly interrupted by a special announcement.

"Hello. I am your Hedonist de la Headmaster. I have accrued those rights that lie in the soft underbelly of small lab animals eaten for consumption. But I digress. Let me have your attention, oh sailors of sanctuary, oh sojourners of suppression. Our counting agencies de la Slime Rot have born me a number. Although the number contains many, many asterisks and notations, and, in fact, counts many things sideways, from right to left, and, in fact, purposefully does not include many things which, if counted, would alter the simple fact I am about to call a fact. Let me simply say that we have a positive credit condition for the first time since our immediate and unrelenting gulping of your credit-converted coin hoarding. That means, people — I say, let us first save, yes, save your future retirements within the cooperation tenements. Yes, yes, that same fund which has been raped repeatedly by all unaccountable, unsavory, and gluttonous members of the Malevolent Seven. Those truly good old boys will now be placed under gold — yes, gold Parchment sprinkles so as to preserve what, to date has yet to be preserved.

"Furthermore, let me announce that our credit-collecting PMF agents, with their long tongues, shall be friendlier. And my own hedonistic tendencies shall be flour for our entertainment yeast, which shall rise, like a new sun, on the electrovision Sunday evening movie screen.

"And finally, with this next gong, I hitherby dub Big Stick Hun our collective Sergeant of Arms. [*gong! gong! gong!*]"

Ferdinand continued to dry heave.

All of a sudden, A.J. yelled, "Shit, I can't get anywhere!"

Constant Love helped Ferdinand to stand up straight. The three of them trotted gingerly to the front of the Parchment Mobile. Outside the front window was a morass of roads, streets, overpasses, tunnels, and bridges so complex and varied that the congestion crews had literally brought the transportation system to a complete and absolute halt. The four of them remained motionless, in the honking and shouting slather of the cement bedlam.

"Damn," said A.J. "I know what this is. I can't believe that I almost forgot. The positioning system on the compubox! It allows you to locate where you are without looking out the window. It's just like the isoblast multiblast. Ferdinand, you were there. The cognitive map, remember?"

Ferdinand stared blankly at A.J.

"Don't you see? The cooperation tenements and the New Tomorrow and yays/nays, you know ... the influence over policy – it's our means of access! All the credits?! Don't you guys see?"

Constant Love stared blankly at A.J.

"The cognitive map *is* the positioning system. Look, in the era of accommodation, the Hedonist or the Malevolent Seven, or whomever — well it's not in their interest to do something that precludes the doing or not doing of something else. Middle of the road, you know? Lip service, wink, wink."

"A.J.," said Ferdinand. "Once again, I have to ask you to get to the point."

Outside, the hapless had begun to circle the psychedelic vehicle. A few were climbing on the hood and pressing their hands and faces against the glass. Some were trying to open the windows and door. Others began to rock the craft from side to side.

"The streets, the roads, all these bridges and tunnels and different ways of crossing Rockville; each one is a physical embodiment of each individual person's political frame of reference. Let's say if Jack, or some other fictitious person —"

"Like The Man With No Name?" interrupted Abbot, sarcastically.

"Yeah, well," continued A.J., "say someone, based on an average of the mental frameworks, or cognitive maps, is left of center or right of center or northwest or southeast, politically, then *his* road looks like that." A.J. pointed to a diagonal road cutting across their path and past a hapless person on the windshield.

"But I almost forgot! To get your road you've got to log on with the positioning system. You've got to enter your name and number. That's how the system reads your mind. Then the congestion crews are dispatched to build your road."

"That's insane," said Ferdinand.

"No, it's perfect," said A.J. "It's the accommodation of all at the expense of everyone — except the Slime Rot."

Ferdinand stared out the window, confused. He let out a deep sigh. "Look," he said. "I don't give a damn about any of that. I just want to get out of here."

Ferdinand looked at Constant Love. "I'm tired of this place. There's a beautiful place, Bonvoyage. I've seen it in my dreams. Come with me."

He looked around. "All of you — come with me. Trust me, it's an amazing place. There's opportunity and hills, and rivers ... you know?"

His eyes pleaded for a spark of optimism. That look alone was enough to make Constant Love feed him an answer of yes.

"How are we going to get out of here?" asked Abbot.

Ferdinand looked around the Parchment Mobile, which was swaying heavily now from side to side.

"A.J., you say we've got guns? No! Wait — there's a better way."

Ferdinand moved to the back of the craft and entered the communication room. The rest of the group followed him inside.

"A.J.?" Ferdinand asked. "You say all I've got to do is punch in my name and number and we'll have the congestion crews out here?"

"Faster than you can say lickety split, captain," said A.J.

"Uh, yeah. Okay, look. I'm going to try something. Wish me luck."

Ferdinand proceeded to log onto the system. First, he wrapped an electrode headband around his temple. Second, he punched in his name.

"Wait," barked A.J. "This will give you your road, but it will also tell the Hedonist and Big Stick exactly where you are! You'll be in the system." He paused to think. "I guess you could just pay that one credit penalty when they show up."

Ferdinand stared at A.J. "We'll have to take that chance," he said.

Ferdinand punched in his number. The electrode headband swelled and pulsed as his eyes twitched. He clenched his fists as the electric pulse accelerated. The positioning system started to blink. Then it began to draw his road.

"Ferdinand, you did it! You did something!" cheered Constant Love.

Ferdinand stepped from the communication room and looked out the window to the west. He walked to the window on the opposite side of the room, and looked out of that also. Nothing. Then, out of the front windshield, past the hapless, he could faintly make out a congestion crew marching toward them.

"They're coming," he stated. "We're leaving. Get ready to go to Bonvoyage!"

8

PRIMORDIAL SLIME

A.J. had long since given up trying to move through the numerous byways and highways of progress and accommodation. The parked Parchment Mobile rocked heavily from side to side. The hapless had surrounded the craft, filling the windows with their gawking, desperate faces.

"Ferdinand, there's no time!" yelled A.J. "The congestion crew is too far away. Even if they could get here in time, they'd probably just congest things even more."

Ferdinand panned his gaze nervously around the craft. "A.J.," he said finally. "Where are the guns?"

A.J. grinned at Ferdinand, then ran quickly into the Enumerated Rights room where he opened a hidden door in the floor.

"Our freedom to kill those who would challenge our abuse of that freedom must be protected," he muttered.

Then, from the front of the craft, they heard glass breaking.

"They're coming in!" A.J. shouted. He pulled various guns and weapons out of the hiding space from underneath the floor, then promptly distributed them to each of the vehicle's inhabitants.

The group stood together holding their guns listlessly while waiting for Ferdinand's instructions. Ferdinand did not move, yet the hapless continued to force their way into the Parchment Mobile.

Abbot suddenly dropped to one knee and began firing methodically into the crowd of hapless now squeezing its way through the broken windshield.

In response, the stunned group moved to the back of the craft.

Abbot turned to them. "Come on!" he screamed.

The windows of the Parchment Mobile began to break away. The arms, legs, hands, heads, and sweaty, determined faces of the hapless jammed their way through the openings in a desperate attempt to gain entrance.

"Don't you get it?" yelled Abbot, firing in all directions. "Only the strongest survive!"

To the horror of all aboard, Abbot continued to fire. As the number of dead hapless multiplied, the surviving hapless slowly began to retreat.

Recognizing the opportunity, Ferdinand turned to A.J. and said, "See if you can move this thing. Drive toward the congestion crew if you can, and close the distance."

A.J. ran to the front. "Cover me," he directed Abbot.

Abbot continued to fire through the broken windows, but high and over the heads of the hapless, so as to provide warning shots to those who might dare make a second attempt.

A.J. made it to the front of the vehicle, pushing dead hapless out of the way to get there. He proceeded to drive the massive Parchment Mobile over everything in its path, living or not.

Abbot cast his weapon aside and moved to the front with A.J.

"Let's see what damage this baby can do," Abbot said, smashing his foot down onto A.J.'s, in turn forcing the accelerator all the way to the floor.

Lurching backward from the sudden acceleration, Ferdinand and Constant Love fell through the door leading to the Enumerated Rights room. As Ferdinand became aware of his surroundings, he was astonished to discover that a group of hapless had boarded the craft, apparently through a trap door underneath the vehicle. Still attempting to gain his balance, Ferdinand raised his gun but did not fire.

"Put that fucking thing down," said one of the hapless men. "We don't want nothin'."

Ferdinand stared at the man, who was dressed in tattered rags. He wore a long, unkempt beard and smelled of sweat and bourbon.

"Put down your weapon then," Ferdinand returned.

"I ain't got no weapon, fool," said the hapless man.

"Turn around then," said Ferdinand.

Then man turned to display a guitar, which hung by a strap from his shoulders and rested against his back. "We play instruments," he said. "We the pleasure for your pain, baby, the lemon for your lime, the inner sanctum eee-vo-lution. We the industrial byproduct, the art for your autocracy, the nameless, faceless voice of freedom crawling from the primordial slime of the Slime Rot."

Ferdinand was stunned. "What?" he asked, incredulous.

The man sang, "A-har har har. Ain't you feelin' it, boy?"

Ferdinand glared silently back. "Okay," he finally said. "You five can stay, but no more. And when I say so, you get off. Understand? You can come to Bonvoyage if you want, but only so long as you don't slow us down."

"We trav'lin'," said the hapless man, "but we ain't necessarily goin' nowhere."

Ferdinand didn't know what to make of it. He walked to the front of the vessel to tell A.J. and Abbot what was going on.

Abbot didn't like the added company but decided against killing the group since they were already aboard and seemed to pose no immediate danger. Meanwhile, the Parchment Mobile continued to roll.

"Look!" said A.J., pointing through the shattered front window. Ferdinand peered ahead to discover the congestion crew closing in and forging an impressive wake in their path. A crew of twelve marched and pulled what appeared to be a giant metal cone.

"Shit!" Ferdinand exclaimed.

"What is it?" A.J. asked.

"It's a giant replica of the Hedonist's cone hat!" exclaimed Abbot. "It must be used as some kind of weapon. Prepare for the fight of your lives, people!"

Abbot grabbed a gun and prepared to fire toward the congestion crew out of the broken, front windshield.

"No, wait!" yelled Ferdinand, hitting Abbot's gun from below and sending the spent rounds through the roof of the vehicle. "Just wait. It'll be okay. I can't believe it, but this might actually work!"

Meanwhile, the group of hapless had begun setting up their instruments in the communication room. Constant Love watched as they started stacking bongos, tuning guitars, blowing into handcrafted wind instruments, and plucking bass strings. They were plugging everything electric into the communication room's control panel, side panels, and customized, rewired, makeshift production panels.

Constant Love drew a pipe from her waistband and sparked some crackle. She offered it to the hapless, each puffing eagerly from the pipe. After they had each had a turn at the pipe, they started to play their instruments. She danced lightly to their jams and was soon handed a tambourine to compliment her moves.

"Mmm ... mmmmmm," said one of the hapless men.

Ahead of the living craft, the congestion crew slowly approached. Pending their imminent arrival, the hapless had scattered from the streets.

"I want you to point this thing directly toward the Abomination House when they arrive," Ferdinand instructed Abbot.

"But that will take us straight to the Hedonist and Big Stick," objected Abbot. "Not to mention Barnacle Row."

"Don't worry about that. We're going to miss it all, and move straight through to Bonvoyage."

Abbot stared at Ferdinand, skeptically. "Ferdinand," he said finally. "You don't know what the fuck you're talking about. You've never even seen any Bonvoyage. I've never heard of any Bonvoyage. And with all these fucking banners and slogans saying *Bonvoyage*, don't you think the Hedonist and all his fucking henchmen would know about it — assuming it exists at all? The problem with you, Ferdinand," he continued, "is that you haven't learned anything about ... about ... logic, and reason, and science. I learned my lessons the hard way, after I was double-crossed by The Man With No Name. You can't just jump out on a flimsy limb, Ferdinand! The survival of the fittest is ordained to those disciplined enough to go through a step-by-step scientific cleansing, not flimsy, whimsy, flatulent faith."

"That's right," said A.J.

Ferdinand glared at A.J.

"The Man With No Name — I mean, X's fall from grace taught me something, Ferdinand," Abbot continued. "It taught me that you have to rely on yourself, your intellect, and your ability to reason and shoot; otherwise, we'd all be a bunch of fucking animals acting by the seat of our stinky emotions all the time."

"That's right," said A.J.

Ferdinand glared at A.J.

"Which are you going to be?" asked Abbot. "A ruthless, merciless, highly evolved soldier of reason or a fucking sheep?"

"Yeah, which one?" asked A.J.

Ferdinand massaged his temples and continued to ignore Abbot.

Finally, he said to A.J., "Just turn this thing toward Barnacle Row." Ferdinand walked to the back of the vessel to lie on the G.R. Board.

Abbot followed after him. "I'm going to prove it to you," he said. "Ruthless research. Pitiless logic. I'll create your perfect world, you emotional little wreck."

Ferdinand muttered, "Good riddance," and walked away to lie down.

Ferdinand drifted off into sleep. The slow, rhythmical rocking and chugging of the Parchment Mobile was too much temptation to resist the comfort of slumber, so there he sank, heavy on the G.R. Board, lost to the world.

FERDINAND'S MIND fell into a heavy, disturbing dream state where Abbot kept reappearing — first, as a dark soldier bent on annihilation, then as a mad scientist in the laboratory of the Parchment Mobile.

Constant Love was there too, dancing and churning in her love groove, moving through the streets of the inner sanctum as a violet ghost, the siren leading lines of dancing, hapless men to the edge of the Outlands.

Abbot appeared in Ferdinand's dream with his face glowing from the green, incandescent hue of the dark laboratory. On the floor beside him were the dismembered parts of the hapless he had killed. Lying lifeless on the table in front of him was the would-be reincarnated body of a creature he had chopped and sewn together. Electricity shot and snapped across the lab. Sparks whizzed by Abbot's face, reflecting in his goggles and arching toward the creature. The compubox monitored the experiment, and Abbot studied the screen with an anxious expression of crazed discovery.

He paced nervously, flipping through various texts, typing on the compubox, inspecting the creature and, finally, throwing the switch. The lab exploded in smoke and fire. Electric currents, like electric blue veins, charged through the creature's face, lighting his eyes with an artificial, steel glow.

"Life!" he screamed. "Give ... me ... LIFE!"

Abbot sat huddled in the corner of his dark lab, looking at his monster with suspicion and awe. Around him, wires were smoking and tubes and bottles were laying in broken pieces on the floor. The creature lay broken and smoking too, until it opened its black mouth and spoke in a horse raspy scream.

"Fer-di-nand!"

FERDINAND AWOKE IN A COLD SWEAT. He woke up coughing and breathless on the G.R. Board. He was in a cloud of smoke, wondering if the entire craft was on fire. The music was so loud that it seemed he had suddenly been transported back in time to the Jalapeño Lounge. He wondered if he was still dreaming.

Gingerly, Ferdinand stepped down from the G.R. Board and set about pulling himself together. He wiped his sweaty face with his shirt-sleeve and, when he felt strong enough to walk, he made his way through the craft, working his way toward the front of the Parchment Mobile.

The vehicle was saturated with noise and smoke. The hapless band, which was now fully electric and wired into the communication room, was sending out long, sonic booms of rhythm and blues, which shook the walls. Ferdinand's head ached. He staggered through the Parchment Mobile to the main room. There he could just make out the figures of Constant Love and A.J. dancing to the music. The floor was littered with bottles and wrappers. Ferdinand pushed on to the front of the craft.

A horrible, high-pitched grinding sound screeched from the front and nearly shook the structure to pieces. To his great disbelief, no one was driving. The front windshield was entirely gone. In its place, an iron plate had been bolted down and welded to the frame.

When Ferdinand heard the drilling and realized they were now underground, he was delighted. This meant that they were already on their way to Bonvoyage. Ferdinand jumped and danced and screamed his way back to the main room where he smashed into A.J. and Constant Love in his excitement. Together they all danced, spinning and hopping to the electric vibrations.

Ferdinand grabbed A.J.'s beer from out of his hand and took a long, hard drink. He sensed, with thirst-quenching conviction, that they were truly on their way this time. He turned to hand the bottle of beer back. When he did, he found himself staring straight into the eyes of Abbot's creature.

The bottle shattered on the floor. Both Constant Love and A.J. stopped dancing right away and the band stopped too. Everyone in the room stood silently, staring at the creature in the middle of the floor.

Abbot moved from the laboratory into the main room to join the onlookers. Abbot's proud grin was madness.

The creature was bald and badly scarred from its head having been stitched and cauterized. With every beat of the thing's heart, some sort of juice would squirt from the fresh head wounds. Its eyes were black, staring at opposite angles; one to the northwest, the other to the southeast. The nose, which did not belong to its face, had been crudely attached. The nose appeared as if it had been broken, repeatedly. The mouth hung open, exposing teeth and gums and a strange-colored drool dripping carelessly down the chin, onto its neck and chest. One of its arms hung precariously backward and seemed to be twitching. Altogether, the creature listed to one side, seemingly as a result of one leg being considerably shorter than the other. Its face was of a dark complexion, its chest brown, with white feet and yellow arms and hands. Its breathing was labored.

Ferdinand turned and threw up.

Abbot walked forward and hugged the creature. The onlooking hapless stood in disbelief. Constant Love and A.J. held on to each other.

Ferdinand wiped the vomit from his mouth and turned to confront Abbot. The creature stared at him as he walked toward them.

"Abbot," Ferdinand said. "What the fuck have you done? What is this thing that you've done?"

"Me?" asked Abbot. "Why, Ferdinand, it should be so obvious! I've created the perfect weapon — the perfect soldier against the increasing bureaucracy of the Slime Rot and the cooperation tenements. Fight fire with fire, I say! Ferdinand, you ask why? Because I have been cleansed. Scientifically cleansed. Simplicity becomes complexity.

"You see, Ferdinand, this is the P.C. Creature. Hacked up and chopped up and sewn back together from a variety of ethnic, social, environmental, gender, and racial backgrounds. The P.C. Creature is the very model of inclusion. Why, this one creature is eligible for no less than 2500 combined credit transfer programs, assistance programs, savings programs, loan programs, insurance programs, training programs, health programs, and contract programs; not to mention Quagmire scholarships, various coupons, and some noteworthy trinkets. This, Ferdinand, is one bad-ass mother fucker."

"Ulllluuuuurrppp!" said the P.C. Creature.

"See, Ferdinand, it speaks seven different languages and fourteen different dialects. In addition, it is tolerant of all races, genders, religions, provinces, origins, and sexual preferences. This, Ferdinand, *is* the collective. We're talking the future Headmaster Hedonist here."

"Ulllluuuuurrppp!" screamed the P.C. Creature.

"Come on, I'll show you," said Abbot. He led the entire crew through the modified lab with its garish display of dismembered hapless, its intricate system of tubes, wires, and redirected electric currents.

"I think," said Abbot, nodding his head, "that the P.C. Creature will be the first citizen of Rockville catapulted into space. Have you heard about that? The Hedonist has announced the impending increase in credit collection to fund the limitless exploration of the vast and limitless wasteland called space. Who better to represent Rockville than the P.C. Creature?!

"And another thing — I know we're underground now, but we're going to have to come up at some point. Have you planned ahead for that? Well, I have. Do you really think they would harm the P.C. Creature? Ha! Impossible! It would be political suicide for them to criticize one hair on this creature's deformed and oversized bald head!"

Abbot stood in his laboratory, triumphant, his hand placed lightly on the leaking head of the P.C. Creature.

"Fuck!" said Ferdinand. Then he turned to leave. "Does this ship have someplace where we can lock up these two maniacs?" he asked A.J.

"Discrimination!" Abbot screamed. "Dis-crim-i-na-tion!!" he screamed again, louder. "I will not put up with this. Oh! Could this possibly be because of who he is? Perhaps its race? Maybe its gender? No way, Ferdinand. No way! I'll turn you in myself if you discriminate against one hair on this creature's stitched head!"

Ferdinand walked out of the lab with the others following close behind. They milled about the craft in disbelief, listening to Abbot and the P.C. Creature bleating pointlessly in the lab.

Ferdinand pulled Constant Love aside. "What's happened?" he asked her.

"What do you mean?"

"With the congestion crew? How did we get here?"

"After you went to sleep, the congestion crew showed up with the filibuster —"

Ferdinand butted in, "— the what?"

"The filibuster. That big drill thing — that's what they call it. They attached it to the front of this thing and covered the windows with iron plates. They pressed some buttons on the positioning system and that's when we started to drill. Why are you asking us about it, Ferdinand? It's *your* road," she pointed out.

"I just wanted to know how it all happened, that's all."

"Well, what did happen, anyway?" Constant Love asked.

Ferdinand turned to address his friends and the hapless musicians.

"Well, when we were stuck back there — when I put on the positioning system headband, I had to think of a way to get out of here. I mean, we couldn't very well escape to Bonvoyage driving down the middle of the street through Barnacle Row! Anyway, the only thing I could think of — I was so mad! So desperate! — was fucking the government right up the ass. Just like they've done to us for so long. I guess it worked; I guess that's why they brought the filibuster. I think we're going straight through to Barnacle Row and the Abomination House, underground. It's my road, all right, but now I'm in the system."

The room was silent.

"Amazing, man," commented A.J.

The hapless returned to their instruments and settled in for the long haul once again. Constant Love and A.J. went to retrieve another beer.

"Get me one, would you?" called Ferdinand. "It's kind of been a rough day. Besides, if Abbot and that creature don't stay in that room, I'm going to need a lot more than just beer to handle all of this."

Constant Love came back with a tray full of items. "Look, Ferdinand. These hapless guys brought all sorts of shit. I mean, we've already got plenty of crackle and caramel right here, but they brought cactus and mushrooms and flowers. Take your pick. We've been having a party the whole time you were asleep. We've got to do something while that fucking filibuster continues to drill — all the noise and smoke! And, who the hell knows what Abbot's going to do? We had no idea he was chopping those dead people into little parts and then sewing them back together again. We just thought he was tidying up a little."

Ferdinand glared at Constant Love.

"Besides," she continued. "We don't really know where this thing's going to stop and what's waiting for us when we arrive. This could be our only time, Ferdinand. Relax! Let fate do the thinking for once."

Ferdinand took a bite of cactus and swallowed some beer. "Sure thing, Love," he said. "Hand me some crackle. Let's go see if Abbot and the P.C. Creature want to party. Fuck it! The more the merrier!"

9

METAMORPHOSIS

"Ulluuurrpp! ULLUUURRPP!"

Ferdinand woke up to the sound of the P.C. Creature screaming.

"Ulluuurrpp! ULLUUURRPP!"

Ferdinand rubbed the sleep from his eyes. He was alone on the G.R. Board in the back of the Parchment Mobile. The room was filled with smoke and a horrible stench. It was difficult for him to see more than a few feet in front of him.

"Creature, what is it?" Ferdinand called out.

"Err ... err ... Ullurrpp!" came the reply.

Ferdinand hastily laced his boots and jumped off of the table. He landed in a thick splash of liquid, soaking his boots and his feet.

"What the hell?" he said to himself. He marched to the front. "A.J.! Abbot! Love! Wake up!"

No one responded.

"Where is everyone?" he thought.

The others slowly started to wake up. The night (or was it day?) had been long and lost. The cactus and flowers and mushrooms and crackle had had their way with them. They were all foggy and smoke-filled, like the interior of their craft.

"Hey, Ferdinand," said A.J. "What's up?"

Ferdinand turned toward the sound of A.J.'s voice. "I don't know. The creature woke me up. He was slurping about something."

"He was slurping something?"

"No. You know, uluurping, or whatever it is that he says."

"About something?" asked A.J.

"Yeah," Ferdinand returned.

"So, you got up? Go back to sleep."

"No," Ferdinand said. "Something's wrong. Look at the floor."

From the couch in the main room, A.J. rolled over to peer at the floor. As his eyes adjusted, he could see that the floor of the craft was filled with a thick, liquid-brown fluid reeking of waste.

"What is it?" A.J. asked, covering his mouth.

"I'm not sure, but I think we're in the sewer system of the Abomination House and the Malevolent Seven. I guess that positioning system took me literally — you know, right up the ass. Anyway, I don't know what these people eat all day long, but it stinks to high heaven and it's rising. We're filling up, A.J. In a few hours? Maybe one hour? I have no idea. We may all drown in the government's shit."

"I can't think of a worse death," said A.J. "You've got to be joking."

"No joke."

"What are we going to do?" A.J. asked.

"I'm not sure. Maybe I can alter our path by putting the positioning system headset on again. I don't know if that's even possible, but it's worth a try. Wake up the others. We've got to prepare to get off the Parchment Mobile. It's going to sink in government waste."

A.J. went to wake the others. Ferdinand marched into the communication room, trying to make heads and tails of the rewired panels. A few of the hapless wandered in and began pulling their instrument wires out and patching the panels back together.

"You've got to make this work," said Ferdinand out loud to himself. "We're all going to die if this doesn't work."

"You going to live forever if it does?" asked the hapless band leader from out of the dark.

"No, but I'm going to get to Bonvoyage. Living there for the rest of my days will be reward enough."

"I think you were in Bonvoyage last night," said the band leader.

Ferdinand stared at the man. "What do you mean?" he asked.

"Never mind," he said.

They each took turns attempting to rewire the positioning system and its incumbent parts, switches, dials, and gears, but to no avail.

Abbot stormed into the room. "Get out of the way! You fools are going to get us all killed! And for what? For what, Ferdinand?" Abbot pushed them out of the room.

"Leave it to a man of science, you idiots! This is a job for a man of theorems and axioms and postulates and tested black-and-white thinking. Leave it to a man who knows how to go about this by utilizing a process, step by step. A man who appreciates and reveres the method!"

Abbot gradually realized that Ferdinand and the hapless man had already left.

In the main room, the hapless had begun stacking their instruments above and away from the wet floor. Ferdinand came over to help them and ran into Constant Love. "Are you all right?" he asked her.

"Yeah, sure," she said. "How are you?"

"Fairly well," said Ferdinand. "I'm tired, though, really tired. And my head hurts. Do you have any caramel balls left?"

"A.J. does." Constant Love replied. "You were really something last night, Ferdinand."

"What do you mean?" he asked.

"You were eating that cactus, and then those flowers. You were spinning around and running and jabbering and laughing and singing. It was fun — I'll give you that! Do you remember any of it?"

"No, not really," he said.

"You kept talking about Bonvoyage," she continued. "And then later, you were drawing and writing some stories and some poetry. You wrote me the sweetest poem, Ferdinand. But, of course you signed it 'Theodore Axehandle.'"

"What do you mean?" he asked.

"You don't remember?"

"No. I guess I don't remember anything," he shrugged.

"Yeah, you were talking about Theodore Axehandle, Man of the People, like it was another side of you, or someone inside of you, or someone you wanted to be — in Bonvoyage."

"Wow! I used to dream I was Theodore Axehandle, Man of the People when I was a kid! I guess I'd forgotten. He was an artist who had these great crimson robes and leather boots and this magical crystal that he wore around his neck. And he had a staff like a wizard's — this magical staff! I guess I've worked for so long in the caramel factory that I'd just forgotten. I grew up, you know? The world took over."

Constant Love stared at him, her eyes maternal. "Here's the poem," she said, handing it to him.

Ferdinand shared a gaze with Constant Love for a moment, then looked down at the poem in his hands.

So long as the turning of the world,
and sounds of machines and their offerings,
So long as I can see and dream,

So long as the clouds cover me and their forms escape me,
So long as my hands feel love and my mouth can taste love,

Until green drips from the maps and dynasties tumble and rest,
and their covenants are written in blood and their souls are sold for heat,

Until water surrounds me and tears fill my pores,
Until I discover the truths told from the wind and her patrons,
Until I fly from here, a spirit moving, as one

So long as I am a man and so long as I can become more,
and so long as there is room for me in heaven,

I will be in love with you.

— Theodore Axehandle

Ferdinand didn't know what to make of it. Finally, he said, "Wow. I guess I kind of made a fool of myself last night."

Constant Love looked at him and laughed. "Don't be silly, Ferdinand. You were great! Really! Here, give it back. I want to keep it. Nobody's ever written me a poem, Ferdinand. I like it. Can I have it back … please?"

Ferdinand handed it back to her. "Anyway," he said. "I've got to get this thing out of the sewer. Look at this place!"

Constant Love looked down. The sewage had indeed risen up to her knees and was quickly filling the craft. "Get us out of here, Ferdinand," she said. "I don't want to die. Not like this."

Ferdinand turned to leave and make his was back into the communication room. "Abbot!" he screamed ahead. "What's taking so long?"

Abbot turned to watch Ferdinand approach. "Nothing's taking so long, Ferdinand. It will work, at least until this shit hits those wires," he said, pointing to a large, twisted conglomeration of spliced wires hanging perilously below the positioning system's panel.

"Okay," said Ferdinand. "Look out. I'm going to try to get us out of here."

"How?" Abbot asked.

"By, uh … amending my previous road. You know?"

"No, I don't, Ferdinand. That positioning system got inside your head, don't you remember? We're driving up the government's sewer because this is who you are — your political frame of reference, Ferdinand. Your anger sent us straight up this shit canal. You can't just change who you are and how you feel about things."

"Well, it's at least worth a try," said Ferdinand.

"Why not let somebody else put on the headset?" asked Abbot. "That will change our path fast enough."

"That won't work," said A.J., stepping into the room. "The filibuster is in motion. The system completes the road before considering another road. Besides, when Ferdinand put on the headset, he identified this craft with him. It has to be Ferdinand. The system won't recognize anybody else."

"All right," said Abbot. "Hurry up, Ferdinand. From the look of things, I'd say we've got about ten minutes before the shit hits those wires."

Ferdinand put on the headset and Abbot threw the switch. The craft immediately jolted and shook. Ferdinand's eyes shut and his neck strained with his thoughts. It appeared as if he were engaged in a battle of wills with the machine collective. He continued to shake as sweat started to bead and then drip down into his face.

"We've got to get him out of there," said A.J. "He can't stand much more of this."

"If this doesn't work, we all die," Abbot reminded A.J. "Leave him alone."

Ferdinand's teeth began to chatter. His eyelids snapped open as if from an electric shock and he clenched his fists very tightly. He shook more violently again and then began screaming in a long crazed howl at consciousness.

"Uhhhh ... rrrrr ... aaahhhhhhh ... AAHHHHHHH!"

The panel started to smoke and spark and the Parchment Mobile suddenly jolted and then began to rise. A.J. snatched the headset from Ferdinand, who collapsed into his arms.

"Ferdinand, you did it!" A.J. yelled. "You did it!"

Abbot was beside himself and close to tears. Constant Love came running into the room and wrapped her arms around both Ferdinand and A.J.

"He did it! He did it!" A.J. exclaimed again and again.

Ferdinand slowly returned to consciousness. He was mumbling.

"What's that?" Constant Love asked. "What's that, Ferdinand?"

Ferdinand waited and breathed in deeply, taking his time. "I ... I ... I ... I pretended I was Theodore Axehandle," he said.

"Who?" A.J. asked.

"You can't pretend on this machine," said Abbot.

"Never mind," said Constant Love. "You did it, Ferdinand. We're getting out of here!"

Ferdinand turned to Abbot. "Fix that machine, Abbot. We're going to need it."

"Why, Ferdinand? Our course has changed," rebutted Abbot.

"Just fix it. Trust me."

"Where are we going, anyway?" asked Abbot.

Ferdinand replied, "Why, Bonvoyage, of course! Didn't you know?"

"You're unbelievable, Ferdinand. As soon as we're above ground, I'm getting off.

Ferdinand exited the communication room. He yelled, "Everyone buckle up! It's going to be a rough landing."

"Ferdinand," said A.J. What's happening? We're picking up speed."

"I know. Hurry up, everyone! We've got about three minutes. You too, Love."

A.J. and Abbot took their seats in the front of the craft, buckling up as instructed. Ferdinand and Constant Love sat behind them. The band of hapless strapped themselves down any way they could. The P.C. Creature was buckled into the electric chair.

"Okay, everyone!" Ferdinand yelled. "If my guess is correct, we're going to explode right through the Slime Rot. I said *through*. We're not stopping, so hold on *tight!*"

Just as Ferdinand finished yelling, the Parchment Mobile burst from the ground and rocketed into the air like a broken intercontinental ballistic missile, which came crashing through the front doors of the Slime Rot. The filibuster, built and powered for drilling through rock, ate up the cement, glass, and drywall of the Slime Rot like lava moving through a jungle.

Slime Rot personnel scattered, running for cover as the Parchment Mobile spewed dust and rock. The monster vehicle churned out shredded walls of paper-stuffed binders in all directions, eating up room after room and building after building as though the very rubble that it produced in its wake was the fuel that fired its locomotion. Inside the machine, Ferdinand was screaming and laughing maniacally.

When the Parchment Mobile finally came to a stop, Ferdinand was ready. He snapped off his shoulder harness and immediately began to mobilize his troops into action.

"We don't have much time," he said.

Just then, a volley of gunfire shot through the vehicle.

Bullets bounced off the iron shields that lay across the windows.

Still other rounds pierced the metal siding, shooting through the body of the craft. Ferdinand and the others took cover on the soggy ground, as the liquid waste drained from the sides of the vehicle.

"Abbot!" Ferdinand yelled. "We need to get the P.C. Creature into the communication room."

"What the hell for?" Abbot yelled back.

"We need him on the positioning system before they shoot it or shoot *us* to hell."

Abbot said nothing in return.

"It'll blow everything!" continued Ferdinand. "The system won't know what to do with him! It won't be able to read his collective cognitive map. We'll blow the whole isoblast multiblast map to shit. The entire grid will go up!"

Abbot nodded his head in agreement. "That just might work, Ferdinand. But I'm not taking the fall for this. This is your bag, Ferdinand. I don't even believe in what you're doing, all right?"

"Fine. Just get him into that headset!"

Abbot crouched forward, then darted quickly to the back, managing to avoid the splattering of bullets shooting through the walls of the craft in the meantime. He quickly unstrapped the P.C. Creature from the electric chair and moved him into the communication room. He placed the headset on the creature. The creature pawed at the contraption. Ferdinand threw the switch.

No response. Nothing. The system was dead.

"Ferdinand," he yelled. "It's no use. It's shorted out!"

Just then, a bullet smashed hot into Abbot's leg.

Abbot screamed and writhed on the floor. "Ferdinand, I've been hit! I'm hit in the leg!" he cried, his voice desperate and weak.

Ferdinand sprang to his feet and ran into the communication room. He crouched down next to Abbot.

"Look," he said. "You're going to be all right. As soon as we get out of here, they'll come in. Blame it all on me. Tell them that I held you and the others hostage. But, you've got to get this to work. We will all die if you can't get the wiring to work. Do you understand me, Abbot?"

Abbot moved under the panel and began cutting and rewiring the positioning system as Ferdinand fashioned a makeshift bandage to slow the bleeding. Bullets flew sporadically through the room as they worked.

"We have to try it," Ferdinand said. "We don't have any more time."

"Just another minute," urged Abbot. "Okay, go!"

Ferdinand reached up and threw the switch. The P.C. Creature's body shot straight and his arms began flapping like a bird.

"Oh shit," said Abbot.

Ferdinand rose to his knees and yelled to the others, "Everybody, GET DOWN!"

The system began shaking the creature from side to side. The lights on the panel were blinking and computing uncontrollably. Sparks flew by as the creature screamed.

"UlluurRRPP!! UlluurRRPP!! UlluurRRPP!

Everything went black.

"Uh oh," said Ferdinand.

All of a sudden, the Parchment Mobile was lifted off the ground from the force of an underground explosion. The craft went through the broken walls of the Slime Rot and came to rest in a cloud of dust and fire. Outside, they could hear the sound of sporadic explosions. Some were very near and others seemed to be some distance away.

Ferdinand peeked through the twisted and smoking frame of the Parchment Mobile. The entire city of Rockville popped and hissed and smoked in splotchy chaos as the positioning grid suffered a smoldering internal combustion.

The system had crashed.

10

BOOTSTRAPS

Ferdinand stepped out of the Parchment Mobile. He could see that the craft had come to rest on a small bluff to the east of the Slime Rot buildings. The buildings lay in ruins, crumbling and on fire, just a few yards away. Further to the west, throughout Rockville, he could see still more fire and, occasionally, small explosions. Below him, the bluff descended along a small embankment until reaching a quagmire of fenced-off refuse and toxic waste. Above him stood the girders and steel tracks of the unfinished Lifeline Rail. The rail speared over the government buildings, cutting across Rockville to the west, stretching in the opposite direction over the toxic waste flats to the east where he could just faintly make out the rail winding its way through the distant mountains of the Outlands.

Constant Love walked toward Ferdinand. "What now?" she asked.

Ferdinand stood there silently, examining the terrain.

A.J. approached from behind. "That was one crazy ride, Ferdinand! I didn't know you had it in you. Hey, look at that shit down there!" he said, pointing to the toxic waste beds. "What's that? More of that government crap?! Why are they keeping that stuff around? Do they want to see what organisms can grow in all that high-priced human manure?"

"Ferdinand," said Constant Love. "We can't stay here. You know they'll be here any minute. What are we going to do?"

"We'll walk to Bonvoyage, like always," he said.

"That's insane," said Constant Love. "We can't walk through the cesspool of waste down there."

"We'll go on the rail," said Ferdinand.

"We can't walk on the rail all the way to those mountains! When will we get there, in a month? What have we got left, Ferdinand, a couple baggies of crackle and two caramel balls," she said, answering her own question. "It's impossible, assuming we could even stay on the rail. Not to mention, Abbot's hurt."

"Somebody will be along for Abbot," Ferdinand assured her. "You know that."

"It's impossible," said Constant Love.

Ferdinand was enraged. He turned to Constant Love and yelled, "We don't have a choice!"

Constant Love said nothing.

"Hey, I'll go," said A.J. "Looks fun to me. Maybe we can slide down the rail, like on our ass the whole way. You know, wwwhh-heeeeeee!"

"A.J.," Ferdinand said. "Gather up our caramel balls and crackle and some rope, or anything else you can think of that we might need. I'll tend to Abbot. We leave in two minutes."

"All right, boss," said A.J.

"I'm sorry," said Ferdinand to Constant Love. I love you. Please help me. I promise something will come along. We'll make it!"

Constant Love looked at him sadly and said, "I'm the one who needs the help. I can't climb up there alone."

"We'll let A.J. go up first and then we'll tie a rope from his waist to yours. He'll pull you up while I push from below. We can do it!"

Ferdinand ran back into the Parchment Mobile and checked on Abbot. He passed A.J. on his way into the thrashed vehicle.

"Ready to go, boss," said A.J.

"Okay, I'll be right out," called Ferdinand.

Abbot lay on the floor, semiconscious. Ferdinand broke off a piece from a caramel ball and handed it to him. Abbot took a bite, then shared the rest with his creature.

"He's in shock, you know," said Abbot, nodding to the creature.

"So are you," said Ferdinand. "Stay down and stay warm. When I get to Bonvoyage, I'll send word."

"Don't," said Abbot. "I wouldn't want to go anyway. There needs to be order, you know. Your destruction of all these Slime Rot regulations will only produce more regulations. How could this happen with all the regulations, anyway? It just shows you we don't have enough. I'm going to do it, Ferdinand. Every aspect of human existence must be regulated. If everyone's out there creating, it's chaos. Creativity must be left to those properly licensed. Permits and fees, applications and approvals.... I'll do it, Ferdinand, I swear."

Ferdinand turned to leave. "Good bye," he said, and walked out. Outside, the band of hapless had their gear in hand, preparing to leave.

"Good luck to you," said Ferdinand.

"No problem, my man," said the hapless bandleader. "More fodder for me larder, if you know what I mean."

Ferdinand didn't. "Which way are you going?" he asked.

"North," the hapless man said. And with that, the group turned and began along the backside of the battle-worn buildings.

Ferdinand jogged down to meet A.J. and Constant Love, who were ready to go. A.J. was wearing a small backpack. He had fastened the rope from his waist to Constant Love's.

"Let's do it," said Ferdinand.

A.J. moved to the nearest truss supporting the rail and began shimmying up a metal pole. He was laboring under his own weight and moving ever so slowly upward. Ferdinand looked behind him to see a small, armed group of tuffies appear from out of the wrecked Slime Rot.

"They're coming," he whispered. "Hurry up."

A.J. worked at the metal poles, his hands and boots digging for traction. Ferdinand boosted Constant Love up the truss where she grabbed tightly and then began to slide down, nearly pulling A.J. off with her.

Ferdinand pushed hard against Constant Love's small boots. A.J.

gathered himself and continued upward. Ferdinand turned to check the tuffies' location. They had just entered the Parchment Mobile.

"Hurry," he urged.

Constant Love had moved far enough along to where Ferdinand could begin climbing. The three inched ever onward, Ferdinand pushing and A.J. pulling, until they reached the top. A.J. grabbed the railing and pulled himself up while Ferdinand supported Constant Love enough to give A.J. needed slack in the rope.

A.J. held out his hand for Constant Love. She lurched forward and missed. She let out a gasping cry as her grip slipped free of the metal, whereupon she dangled precariously from the rope, swinging freely from side to side. She screamed. Ferdinand reached out and grabbed her, covering her mouth as two tuffies exited the Parchment Mobile and hiked down the embankment to search the area beneath them.

Constant Love held on to Ferdinand. A.J. held on to the rope. Ferdinand held his breath. The tuffies scanned the area around them, but did not think of looking up. Not seeing anyone, they hiked further down the hill to the fenced-off wastelands. They peered through the fence where the pools of toxic waste bubbled up and steamed in the afternoon sun. One of the tuffies fired a volley of shots through the fence. Finally, they walked back to the Parchment Mobile.

As soon as the tuffies stepped into the Parchment Mobile, A.J. once again started to pull Constant Love up with the rope with Ferdinand pushing her from behind. Constant Love grabbed the metal track and, with the help of A.J., pulled herself up and on top. Constant Love and A.J. collapsed onto one another, panting for air.

Ferdinand followed closely behind, joining his two friends, where the three rested together. They lay along the track and watched the Parchment Mobile be towed away. Three of the tuffies remained behind and stood watch along the edge of the ruined buildings.

"What are we going to do all night?"

"Well," answered Ferdinand, "at least the tuffies won't be able to spot us."

"What about sliding down this rail?" asked A.J.

Ferdinand ignored him. "Let's wait and see," he said. "Maybe something will come up."

With the tuffies standing watch, the three crawled forward, hugging the railing as the evening sun set behind them. When they determined they were far enough away and that it was sufficiently dark to walk without being detected, they stood up and began walking, very carefully, along the eastbound track toward the Outlands.

After a number of blocks, they grew tired and were forced to stop. They huddled close together and tied themselves to the metal track in order to secure themselves, in the event that they fell asleep. The waste glowed and bubbled below.

"That's amazing," said Constant Love.

"Yeah, real purty," said A.J.

"This goes on for blocks," said Ferdinand. Below them the land glowed, green and blue and blue-green and yellow and red and orange. Like fields in the spring, the toxic waste almost seemed manicured and ready to harvest. Above them, the moon shined full.

"I don't feel good," announced Constant Love. "I'm cold."

"Here," said A.J. "Have some crackle."

Constant Love puffed deeply on the pipe that A.J. had handed to her. Ferdinand and A.J. followed and then the three hungrily devoured their last caramel ball.

"I'm scared," admitted Constant Love. We're blocks and blocks from those mountains, Ferdinand. We'll never make it. I'm too weak to go on. I don't even know if I can make it back."

Ferdinand stared off into space, the rainbow colors of the dark landscape reflecting in his eyes. He kept silent.

They sat there, huddled together.

Suddenly, A.J. whispered, "Hey, listen!"

The sound of a rolling railcar seemed to be coming from the east.

"It's coming our way," warned A.J.

Ferdinand's eyes opened and his heart leapt. Constant Love was too delirious to care much about what was going on.

"A.J.," he said. "We've got to get that car."

"How?" A.J. asked.

"I don't know. We've got to stop it. We've got to get that car."

"Ferdinand," said A.J. "It will be here any second. It's coming too fast!"

Ferdinand untied himself and crawled over to the westbound side of the track where he proceeded to lay across the steel rails.

"Give me the rope!" he said. "Tie me on! Quick!"

"Ferdinand, you'll die! That's insane. You'll die for certain!" Constant Love screamed.

Ferdinand was crazed and determined. "Just tie me on by the time it gets here!" he screamed to A.J.

A.J. worked feverishly to free the rope, as the sounds of the approaching railcar grew louder. He managed to untie the rope, first from around Constant Love's waist, then from the Lifeline Rail itself. He held one end firmly in his hand. The other end remained fastened about his waist. A.J. crawled over to the westbound track and wrapped the rope around Ferdinand.

Ferdinand screamed. "There's no time!"

The railcar roared ahead of them, now just twenty yards away.

"There's no time!" A.J. repeated as the car smashed into Ferdinand, knocking him off the track. At the same time, A.J. jumped back, away from the car, falling helplessly over the edge.

Constant Love screamed in horror as the car turned end over end along the rail, eventually screeching to a stop some thirty yards from her down the western side of the track.

"Ferdinand!" she screamed. "Ferdinand!"

"I'm down here!" he yelled, to her disbelief.

"So am I," yelled A.J.

Ferdinand and A.J. dangled over the opposite sides of the track, suspended by the rope, each held firmly in place by the weight of the other.

"If we both pull at the same time, we can climb up together," said Ferdinand.

The two lifted their bodies precariously up the rope in unison, while Constant Love looked on in amazement. As they reached the top, the two friends grabbed onto one another, secure on top of the track once more. They gasped for air.

"Now," said Ferdinand between breaths. "Let's get that car."

Ferdinand and A.J. walked down a ways and hoisted the car onto the eastbound side of the track.

"It's full of crackle!" yelled A.J.

There, at the bottom of the car, snug under the seat, rested four large bags of crackle.

"Well, I'll be damned," said Ferdinand. "Look!"

Below them, bubbling in the orange glow of the toxic waste sank the remaining bags of crackle, which had been thrown from the railcar. They watched as the liquid waste consumed the large crystalline mound.

Ferdinand interrupted the silence. "Let's get to those mountains!" he said.

Constant Love climbed into the railcar. Ferdinand and A.J. gingerly pushed the car along the eastbound track until it had picked up some speed, then they jumped in with their female companion.

"We're moving now!" Ferdinand screeched, as the wind pushed back his hair from his face. For the first time in days, he felt the sense of freedom and impending paradise of Bonvoyage.

"Ferdinand," Constant Love yelled. "How are we going to stop? The track isn't supposed to be completed yet."

"I don't know," said Ferdinand. "But it's better than walking."

The railcar picked up momentum as it raced faster and faster through the strange darkness toward the mountains. Over the track, at intermittent intervals, the railcar sailed beneath various large signs, which read WARNING, YOU ARE ENTERING THE OUTLANDS — BEWARE THE INTERLOPERS.

"I don't like the looks of this," said Constant Love. "They must know we're coming. We don't have anything to defend ourselves with against the interlopers, Ferdinand."

"We'll be all right," responded Ferdinand. "We've made it this far. We can't turn back now. Besides, I'd like to meet somebody new."

The railcar continued to pick up speed until, under the full moon, the mountains made themselves known.

"We'll be there in no time," said Ferdinand.

"I hope this track doesn't end at the Outlands," said A.J. "I don't see any tunnel."

"You couldn't see it even if there was one. Besides, there's got to be one. Somebody filled up this car, didn't they?"

"Unless they're using this unfinished track for their own smuggling," said A.J.

"Here they come!" screamed Constant Love, abruptly.

Indeed, the mountains had filled their vision, yet they continued to pick up speed.

One hundred ... seventy ... thirty ... ten yards away.

"We're going to crash right into them!" she screamed.

Now all of them were screaming in mad panic as the railcar raced into and then through the mountains, whereupon they found themselves falling desperately downward and off of the track, crashing into a body of water below.

FERDINAND FOUND HIMSELF FUMBLING UNDERWATER, nearly out of air. The great distance of his fall had submerged him deep under the surface and he had lost his sense of direction. In a final attempt for life he blew out the last of his air and, with the palm of his hand, he felt the bubbles rise. He used his remaining strength to follow the bubbles to the surface.

As Ferdinand approached the top, he unexpectedly felt someone grab onto his baggies and pull him up and out of the water. It was A.J., who helped him onto the shore where Constant Love was buckled over and breathing desperately for air.

They all remained there for some time, resting. A.J. moved between Ferdinand and Constant Love and drew the two near him for warmth. They fell asleep on the banks of the water, wrapped together.

11

BRUTALITY

Ferdinand was the first to awaken in the morning. The bright sunlight warming his face greeted his consciousness, which accepted the invitation to enlightenment. He opened his eyes, straining and squinting against the bright sun. He felt his limbs, which were all accounted for, and sat up, pulling hard against his sore muscles. He could not remember ever having been so physically exhausted.

Rather than waking the others, he elected to explore the surroundings a little. As his eyes began to focus, he could see before him the body of water in which they had landed. It was a large reservoir surrounded by bags of sand. His eyes moved up to the track, which simply ended in midflight over the reservoir. The track jutted through a round opening in a wooden wall. He followed the outline of the wall and discovered that it was supported by wooden beams. Ferdinand realized that the mountains which he had viewed from the bluff had simply been a pictorial backdrop that they had soared through in their iron railcar, the backside of which he was now viewing.

His heart sank.

He looked to the left and then to the right. Ferdinand could just make out what appeared to be a massive industrial complex of endless factories, hidden behind the mountainous backdrop. He couldn't believe it. The closest factory stood directly along the eastern shore of the reservoir.

Ferdinand walked along the reservoir's banks until he reached the structure. He climbed over an enclosing fence and then shimmied up the outside of the factory by climbing on the uneven rock wall.

As he wound his way up, he was able to obtain views of the inner workings through the factory windows. There he saw the conveyor belts and stores of industrial ingredients which, multiplied a hundred-fold by the surrounding factories, undoubtedly were the makings of a monumental sum of crackle.

In a flash, he understood it all. The Lifeline Rail, connecting Fern Lane to Barnacle Row and the so-called Outlands (this industrial complex) was, in essence, a massive transportation system for the government's crackle to all the provinces of Rockville. The Hedonist's staunch denials, followed by the compromised deals with the PMF Angels, the Quagmire, the Slime Rot, the Malevolent Seven, the tuffies, and The Man With No Name were evidence of a collusive effort at the top levels of official and sociological governing; Weasel Salsa's skepticism over the amounts and the source of the crackle, Big Stick's buy off of the Headmaster Hedonist, and even the planned development for the cooperation tenements. All of it made sense. It all pointed to communal addiction, wealth transfers, and population control.

Ferdinand climbed down, despondent. He looked down the row of factories but could see nothing else in sight. He walked back to his friends, who were still sleeping.

"Wake up," he said. "Wake up!"

Constant Love and A.J. opened their eyes briefly, then rolled back over.

"Wake the fuck up!" Ferdinand screamed.

Constant Love shot up straight, sitting on the ground. "What is it?" she asked.

"It's more like, 'What *isn't* it'," Ferdinand replied.

Constant Love waited. Meanwhile, A.J. slowly awoke. Ferdinand, explaining their surroundings, described what he had seen. Finally, he offered that they go back and attempt to blend in within the inner sanctum.

"I bet those band guys would put us up," suggested A.J.

Constant Love alone remained resolute. "What are you talking about, Ferdinand? We can't go back! There's nothing to go back to! You said so yourself before we left. We've just survived the most incredible events I can imagine to come this far. *So what* if we've landed here? We're halfway, Ferdinand. We have to be! This can't go on forever. No one needs that much crackle! There's got to be something on the other side of this wasteland. You wanted to go to Bonvoyage, Ferdinand, not the Outlands. So, let's get up and start walking — to Bon-voy-age!"

Ferdinand's eyes opened wide again as he gazed at the horizon. "Of course," he said. "It's further. We keep going. You're right. You're right. This is nothing — just more of the same. It's further."

Ferdinand pointed east, even further east, to Bonvoyage.

The companions gathered themselves and started walking again. Constant Love sparked the crackle and they smoked. The brazen rock, which fixed their eyes open, now seemed stacked in horrific monuments all around them.

Ferdinand thought, "Later, I'll eat those buttery vegetables and drink from that clear, clear stream ... the ice caves and the roasted fish and singing birds ... and Constant Love, yes! Her body wet from a light perspiration, and olive green, like her eyes. Oh, I'll wrap myself inside her and taste life again!"

They walked on. The dirt roads were deserted. The factories appeared to run automatically. They hadn't seen another single person.

They continued to walk into the next day and the next. The reservoirs provided plenty of water, but their hunger was increasing. The crackle had left them jittery and weak.

Without warning and all at once, there in the street someone was coming toward them. He had a dog with him.

Ferdinand gestured for them to run and hide around the next corner, but Constant Love was too weak to run. Weaker still, A.J. tripped on something in the road and fell down. Constant Love dropped to her knees and pleaded for A.J. to get up. Ferdinand, committed not to leave his friends, turned around and waited for the impending arrival of the stranger.

"Perhaps he could even help us," Ferdinand thought.

A large man in grey work baggies approached, smoking as he sized them up. An old mutt hump panted happily and lazily by his side.

"What you do'n here?" he called out.

Ferdinand looked at the man and replied, "Heading through — we're moving through ... east."

"Oh," was all the man said in return.

"Who are you?" asked Ferdinand.

"I work in the factories. We all do."

"We haven't seen anyone else," Ferdinand returned.

"That's because we're not let out. We're all prisoners here, transferred from the hemphouse."

"You mean the suicides are really transfers?" Ferdinand asked.

"No," said the man. "Most are suicides, but some are transfers."

"What are you doing out?" Ferdinand asked.

"My job is to make sure nobody else is out. See this eye?" he said.

Ferdinand squinted up into the midday sun, shielding his eyes with his hands. He could just make out his own glassy reflection in the man's eye.

"They had my eye surgically replaced with this," he said pointing to the glass eye. "It's a camera. I just walk around and everything's sent back to the main office. You're on camera. If you're not supposed to be out here, they'll know and come get you. I just walk around."

With that, the man began heading down the street behind the group.

"Wait!" Ferdinand yelled after him. "Which way to Bonvoyage? Which way, east? Where does this end?"

The man turned. "You're almost there," he said. "Few hundred yards east, you'll hit the wall."

"Let's go!" Ferdinand screamed. "One last hurdle!"

"Wait!" cried Constant Love. "Mister, can I have a hit of that crackle?"

"This ain't crackle!" the man screamed. "I don't smoke that shit! It's hemp. I'm smoking hemp. It helps me relax and dream. That's one thing I still have. Bonvoyage." He sighed. "I smuggled the seeds out of that hemphouse. I've got a little stored over the wall there. Here, take one," he said, and handed one to Constant Love.

"Thanks," she said, disappointed. She slipped the seed into her filthy baggies.

"Let's go!" said Ferdinand. "Come on!"

Ferdinand started to jog east, with the others following, slower, behind him.

"We haven't got much time," he screamed. "They've seen us!"

It wasn't long before Ferdinand could faintly see the outline of a wall.

"There it is!" he screamed. "I see it! I see it!"

A.J. and Constant Love doubled their speed with Ferdinand's good news. They soon caught up to him, and the three of them began running now, stride for stride together, toward their long-sought freedom.

Ferdinand reached the wall first. It stood above him towering at least twelve monstrous feet high. It was a cement block wall, much too thick to smash through. The wall was painted a light grey, matching perfectly to the surrounding dirt streets and grey factories of the supposed Outlands.

To the left, they could see nothing but wall. To the right, about fifty yards to the south, was what appeared to be a guard tower, and then more wall.

"What are we going to do?" asked Constant Love.

"We're going to climb this wall," said Ferdinand.

"How?" asked A.J., simply.

Ferdinand was stumped. He figured it would take at least two people to boost one person to the top of the wall and then, even if that worked, it would take a miracle for the first person to hang down low enough to pull up the second person. At a minimum, one person would be left behind.

"We'll have to break through the guard tower," Ferdinand said. "Let's go."

Ferdinand, Constant Love, and A.J. jogged south to the guard tower. There in the wall hung a locked, metal door adjacent to a metal booth, which was manned by a ranger.

"Good afternoon, sir," greeted Ferdinand. "We've come to go east. That's our plan."

"Good afternoon," the ranger greeted back. "No problem, no problem. I'll just need to see your Wilderness Permit."

"Our what?" Ferdinand asked.

"Your permit, your Wilderness Permit."

"We haven't got a permit," Ferdinand said. "What's a Wilderness Permit? Why the fuck do we need a permit to go into the wilderness?"

"Because," explained the ranger, "if too many people go into the wilderness, then plants get crushed and forest fires start and people get lost. It's a fragile area, son, and we the people have to regulate how many of us can travel into the wilderness, for those reasons."

Ferdinand was stunned. "What about all that fucking toxic waste, you asshole?"

"Well," said the ranger. "We need more regulations."

"Look," Ferdinand said. "Where do we get this permit? Can we get it from you?"

"No, no, no, no, no, no. No!" said the ranger. "Ministry of Permits. That's the place. Come back with your permit and then I'll let you through — after 24 hours."

To the north, Ferdinand could just make out a small group of people heading toward them. They appeared to be tuffies. Ferdinand looked above the booth, detecting a camera perched on the wall.

"We don't have time for this," he said. Ferdinand reached into the booth, where he proceeded to choke the ranger.

"Give me the keys to the wall or I'll kill you!" he screamed in the ranger's face.

The ranger could barely speak. "I ... haven't ... got ... the ... keys," he said.

Ferdinand loosened his grip.

"Why not?"

"Because I've never seen anyone with a permit. I've never needed the keys before."

Ferdinand sank to his knees. "How long have you worked here?"

"My whole life. I took one of those tests at the Quagmire, you know, with the bubbles? I kept filling in answers that indicated I wanted to be my own boss and work outdoors. Anyway, believe it or not, it said I should be a ranger. So, here I am. The only ranger in Rockville!" the ranger said proudly.

"Ferdinand, they're getting closer," warned Constant Love.

"Okay," said Ferdinand. "A.J., you lift Love on your shoulders and lean her toward the wall. I'll climb up you and Love to get to the top. When I'm on top, I'll hang down and pull Love up. Then we'll grab a branch from the other side and pull you up with it, A.J. Okay?"

"Okay, boss," said A.J.

A.J. hoisted Constant Love onto his shoulders. Constant Love stood up, leaning against the wall. Ferdinand jumped onto A.J. and began climbing up his lover. At this point the tuffies were now sprinting toward the ranger station.

They're coming!" Constant Love screamed. "Hurry! Hurry!"

The tuffies were now just yards away.

"Ferdinand, hurry!!!"

Ferdinand threw one hand on top of the wall, then the other. He pulled himself up to the point where his eyes could just about clear the cement barrier and see into Bonvoyage when he felt Constant Love fall away, and he was forced violently to the ground.

Ferdinand landed hard, but quickly scrambled away from the clutches of the tuffies and broke into a run, heading further to the south. He looked back and saw that Constant Love and A.J. were now in the custody of the tuffies.

Ferdinand stopped abruptly in his tracks and grabbed a rock off the ground. The tuffies drew their guns. Desperately, he turned to run again, but abruptly stopped at the wall instead. He began scratching Bonvoyage into the cement with the rock.

The tuffies immediately seized Ferdinand, dragging him backward with them. His face streamed with the tears, sweat, and dirt of his paradise lost.

12

PRINCIPLES

F erdinand found himself gagged and bound, secured safely away deep inside the hemphouse. The Slime Rot regulations droned on.

"Section 703(c)(II)(B)(1) of the Rockville Penal Code states that all vasectomies shall be performed in accordance with the following calibrated measurements, to wit: (1) Upon the placement of the vasectomy order with a Rockville approved technician, said technician shall submit the pink copy of such order to the Measurement's Council, which shall, in concert with the state-approved Measurement's Body, either stamp the pink copy "Green Go Ahead" or "Red No Go," provided such Measurement's Body has consulted with the technician prior to such stamping or has otherwise established, through regulations, the preapproved measurement intervals for vasectomy cutting and has published those intervals either in the Code of Regulations or with a periodical (i) located within 50 blocks of the applicable morgue and/or technician cutting and (ii) with a distribution of at least 100,000 people per three-week frame of time."

Ferdinand was struggling to hang himself when Weasel Salsa approached his cage.

"Hi, Ferdinand," he said.

Ferdinand mumbled and struggled.

"They said I could find you here. I'm your instigator."

Ferdinand mumbled and struggled.

"I know, you thought I was dead — bullshit *Slanted View*."

A guard walked up and motioned for Ferdinand to come over. The guard cut the gag from Ferdinand's mouth.

"I can't believe it's you!" said Ferdinand. "I thought for sure you were dead. Lift me up so that I can hang myself."

"No, no, no, no, no, no, no," said Weasel. "We're going to let the system work, Ferdinand. Law and order, you know?"

"Since when did you become an instigator?" asked Ferdinand.

"While you were away."

"I thought it took longer than that," said Ferdinand.

"Correspondence courses," replied Weasel.

"Oh," Ferdinand concluded.

"Anyway, I'm doing this because I thought I could help. That, and I feel somewhat responsible for you getting caught up in all this."

"Do I have a chance?" Ferdinand asked.

"No, you don't," said Weasel.

"They're going to electrocute me, then?"

Well, usually that's what they would do, but they have another idea in mind for you, Ferdinand. You see, they've started this space program. They want to explore the space up there, you see? So, they've built this ridiculous, giant catapult to launch the P.C. Creature as Rockville's ulti-mate representative into space, but they haven't tested it. They've tested it with monkeys — apparently with success because the monkeys haven't come back yet. Now they need a human test subject. Anyway, they've rewritten the laws for capital punishment to include death by catapult. You see, Ferdinand, you may get to Bonvoyage after all."

"That's great, Weasel," Ferdinand said, sarcastically.

"Yeah, I thought so. The trial is today, at 2:00. They're not fooling around here. The Headmaster himself is going to act as the judge and Big Stick, as Sergeant of Arms, is the prosecuting instigator."

"Do I get a jury?"

"Yes and no," said Weasel. "The P.C. Creature is going to act as the jury since it represents the mind of the collective in any event."

"And let me guess," said Ferdinand. "If it says 'uulluurrpp,' that means guilty, right?"

"How'd you know, Ferdinand?"

"Lucky guess. Where's Constant Love?"

"Both her and A.J. are here in the hemphouse. They're refusing to testify against you for the plea bargains. Abbot's their main witness. He sang like a canary."

"Listen, Weasel," said Ferdinand. "If you do nothing else, I want you to make certain that they both testify against me for those plea bargains. I want them free. That fucking creature will convict me either way, it doesn't matter. You make sure those two go free, understand?"

"Yeah, sure," agreed Weasel. "Okay."

"What else is Abbot doing?"

"You wouldn't believe it, Ferdinand. The Hedonist really likes that P.C. Creature. They rewarded Abbot by giving him the bureaucratic job of his choice. He picked Head Regulator. He's regulating everything. He's even regulating how things should be regulated! They call it 'procedural regulations.' The Slime Rot has doubled in size since you tore through it with that filibuster. He's going to have a lot of weight, politically, as the creator of that P.C. Creature."

"After I'm convicted — hey, what am I charged with, anyway?"

"Crimes against the state, like treason and failing to pay that overdue penalty credit on your insurance bill."

Ferdinand sighed. "Okay. After I'm convicted, when will I be catapulted?"

"Tomorrow morning," said Weasel pointedly. "They're not fooling around here."

"What else is there to know?" Ferdinand asked.

"Not much. The press is going crazy, of course. *The Slanted View* is printing all sorts of crap. Here," Weasel said, handing Ferdinand a paper from out of his briefcase.

Snap. Crackle. Pop. That's the sound of the new justice catapult, which will soon send Ferdinand into that great Bonvoyage. Like cereal floating in milk, this saga of treason and more treason has become saturated with the truth. "I did it," stated a man who looks alarmingly like Ferdinand. "I did it and I'm glad I did it," he said again, when we asked him if he was sure. Never before has Rockville seen such cowardly avarice spewed with such bravado. "Why'd you do it?" we asked. The answer, "For the money." Good enough for us.

"Unbelievable," commented Ferdinand.

"I know," said Weasel. "That look-alike joker's doing interviews, too. He's here every day. It's amazing. Anyway, you'd better get ready, the trial's in one hour."

Ferdinand nodded his head affirmatively and closed his eyes.

"HEAR YE, hear ye, the High Court of Rockville is now in session, the honorable Headmaster Hedonist presiding. All rise!" said the bailiff.

Everyone rose as the Headmaster Hedonist, dressed in traditional black robes and wearing the silver cone hat and bandit's mask, marched into the courtroom. He sat down and smashed the gavel against the desk.

"Be seated and come to order," commanded the bailiff.

Ferdinand sat next to Weasel. His arms and legs were bound. At the opposite table sat Big Stick Hun, who was staring at Ferdinand with a wry smile. Behind Big Stick sat Penelope. The P.C. Creature was sitting in the jury box, bound to his chair with hemp rope and wearing a bib to absorb the drool, which spilled from his mouth and dripped from his chin.

"What is Penelope doing here?" Ferdinand whispered to Weasel.

"She's with Big Stick now," Weasel whispered back. "They've been together ever since you guys broke away from your hovel. When she came looking for you, Big Stick took her hostage. They've been together ever since."

Ferdinand heaved a sigh.

"People, I am the Headmaster Hedonist. I am in control here. Only I know all rules and other things. Here, people, I am the rule maker and you are the rule taker. I shall make the prosecution's opening statement now."

"Objection!" yelled Weasel. "Your honorable Hedonist, it is not your place to —"

"Silence!" interrupted the Hedonist, smashing the gavel down on the podium before him. "One more objection from you, Weasel, and I'll have you arrested."

Weasel sat down.

The Headmaster Hedonist continued. "My opening statement: Guilt? What is guilt? Guilt is like the bosom of a young woman fresh from the laundry, filled with the perfume of creams and passion. Wander with me, people, to a place filled with such lusty, sinful passions."

He smashed the gavel down again.

"A bed, if you will, laden with guilty, young girls ... and boys. I'm terrible! I'm terrible? No!" The Hedonist smashed the gavel down again.

"People, such is the lustful nonsense of fairy tales. For our great populace has been raped—"

He struck the gavel down again.

"—by this defendant, Ferdinand, simply to line his own pockets!

He struck the gavel down again.

"He is your Judas! He is your Brute! He is your Spartacus! I ask only that you bring back a verdict of guilty. Thank you."

He struck the gavel down three times.

"Now, Weasel. You may submit your opening statement in writing to the clerk of the court, for the record, following my verdict — and no more objections!"

He struck the gavel down once again.

"Big Stick, you may call your first witness."

"The prosecution calls Abbot to the stand, your high eminence," said Big Stick.

Abbot walked to the stand and sat down.

"State your name for the record," said Big Stick.

"Abbot," said Abbot.

"Thank you. Now, in your expert opinion, sir, is the defendant guilty as charged?" Big Stick asked Abbot.

"Objection!" screamed Weasel.

"Arrest that man," ordered the Hedonist. "Counsel, I warned you not to object again. I am holding you contemptible. You may finish this trial, but you shall now be bound and gagged."

The bailiff moved quickly behind Weasel and bound his arms and legs. He then tied a rope around his mouth, which Weasel promptly bit down upon.

"I'll repeat the question," said Big Stick.

Abbot piped in, "That's okay. I hear you. The answer is yes. Yes, he is. Which is, in fact, the opposite of no, no he isn't. But let me tell you that this type of direct answer and question goes against regulations. Regulation 46(c)(d)(A) of the Rockville Code of Regulations specifically prohibits any type of direct question that elicits a yes or no answer from anybody, whether it be your average man or woman on the street or me, sitting in this chair."

"That's fine. Thank you," said Big Stick.

"Call your next witness!" the Hedonist screamed.

Abbot left the courtroom. As he passed Ferdinand, Abbot gave him a big wink.

With a furtive grin, Big Stick said, "The prosecution calls Constant Love to the stand."

Constant Love walked up to the stand and sat down.

Big Stick leaned slyly on one elbow as he addressed the stand. "Now, Constant Love. Isn't it true that you're a cheap whore?"

"What?" screamed Constant Love. "Fuck you!"

The Hedonist laughed. "Okay. Okay," he said between snorts. "Good work, Big Stick. Good work. Very nicely done. Love, you may leave the stand. Big Stick, call your next witness."

Constant Love left the courtroom. She was holding back tears as she walked out, her gaze fixed on Ferdinand.

"The prosecution calls A.J. to the stand, your most highly Hedonistic Headmaster."

The Hedonist continued to laugh. "Yep. Damn!" More laughter came from the Hedonist.

A.J. walked to the stand and sat down.

"Are you not A.J.?" Big Stick asked of him.

"I am that which you portend, my pithy prosecutor," said A.J.

"How so?"

"So? So large and magnanimous that it shall suffice to say 'Bonvoyage' my rotund, redundant one."

Big Stick stared at A.J. "Dismissed. The prosecution rests."

A.J. left the courtroom, giving Ferdinand a wink as he walked past.

The Hedonist spoke. "Okay. Okay, Weasel. I'm in a good mood. So, I'm going to let you make a closing statement. Bailiff! Ungag his mouth!"

"Thank you, Hedonist. Your honor, creature of the jury, I have just one word and one word only." Weasel looked at the creature and screamed.

"Uuulluuurrpp!! Uuulluuurrpp!! Uuulluuurrpp!!"

Upon hearing the screaming chant, the creature started to scream with excitement in return. "UUULLUUURRPP!! UUULLUUURRPP!! UUULLUURRPP!"

The creature pulled at the restraints holding him down, jumping and hopping and screaming with excitement.

"UUULLUUURRPP!! UUULLUUURRPP!! UUULLUURRPP!"

"Silence!" yelled the Hedonist.

The creature kept on screaming.

"What did you do that for?" asked Ferdinand.

Weasel replied, "I'm trying to get it hoarse, so that it can't say 'guilty.'"

"Good thinking," said the defendant.

"Uulluurrpp!!" sang the creature, again and again.

The Headmaster screamed, "Put a bag over its head!" He announced to the court, "Since it's screaming 'guilty' over and over again, we might as well move to sentencing. Do you the jury, P.C. Creature, find the defendant, Ferdinand, guilty of the crime of treason?"

The P.C. Creature suddenly stopped in mid yell, shutting its mouth with a quick snap. It stared straight ahead, completely silent.

"Fuck, I think it worked," whispered Weasel.

"Okaaayyyy," said the Hedonist. "Big Stick, you wanna get that creature some water?" And get Abbot in here with those electrodes."

Big Stick returned with Abbot and an array of horrible equipment.

"Let's get this creature to talk, Abbot," said the Hedonist.

Abbot placed the electrodes on the creature and threw the switch. Its body jolted and smoked, but no words were uttered. Again and again the experiment ran, but the P.C. Creature remained steadfast.

"That's remarkable," said Ferdinand.

The Headmaster continued. "Moooving on. Do you the jury, said P.C. Creature, find the defendant, Ferdinand, guilty of the charge of refusing to pay the overdue penalty credit arising from the late payment of his insurance bill?"

"ULLUURRPP!!" came the response.

"Perfect," said Weasel. "Why didn't you just pay it, Ferdinand?"

"I did," said Ferdinand. "I dropped it in the mail three days before it was due. I guess it took four days to get there. Am I responsible for estimating the speed and efficiency of the Rockville delivery system? It's the principal of the matter."

Weasel stared at him in disbelief.

Ferdinand turned to the gallery and made eye contact with Penelope. She stuck her tongue out at him. Constant Love was nowhere in sight. He turned back around to face the Hedonist, who was speaking.

"Being found guilty of payment refusal and overdue with willful malfeasance, the State sentences you to be catapulted tomorrow morning. Case dismissed."

The bailiff moved to take Ferdinand away. Ferdinand said, "Here," as he handed Weasel a note. "Give this to Constant Love. And one more thing — get me an interview, an exclusive, with that Ferdinand look-alike tonight. I want to give him my side of the story."

"Will do," promised Weasel.

Ferdinand was taken away. As he was dragged down the hall, he could still hear the P.C. Creature yammering "Uulluurrpp" in the distance.

13

BONVOYAGE

Ferdinand lay on the floor of his hemphouse cage thinking about what the man in the Outlands had told him about hemp and his plants outside the wall.

"Hey, Ferdinand," said Weasel, suddenly appearing before his cage.

"Hey, Weasel. What's new?" Ferdinand returned.

"I gave that note to Constant Love, like you asked. She read it, and she said she understood."

"Good," said Ferdinand.

"And that look-alike guy, he'll be here at 9:00, alone."

"Perfect," said Ferdinand.

"Constant Love also gave me these for you."

Ferdinand watched Weasel reach through the hemphouse ropes and dump a pile of crimson robes on the floor of his cage.

"What's that all about?" asked Weasel.

"Never mind," said Ferdinand. "It's a long story."

"Okay, well look, if you need anything, let me know," said Weasel. "I'll wait here with you until morning, if you want."

"No, that won't be necessary. Thanks anyway, though," said Ferdinand.

"All right. Oh, I almost forgot! A.J.'s started an underground paper.

He's calling it *Bonvoyage*. You know how he likes those conspiracy theories about everything: gaming sheets, instigators, technicians, all that shit. Well, it's all there, Ferdinand. He's already started printing and distributing the thing. One issue and they're already looking for him. I guess that's what all that nonsense was on the stand today."

Ferdinand laughed. "That's great. Just great. What about Abbot? What was all his winking about?"

"I have no idea," said Weasel, who turned and walked away.

FERDINAND LAY BOUND by his feet and arms on the floor of his cage, waiting for his look-alike to arrive. At 9:00, his visitor appeared and was led into Ferdinand's cage. The two were left alone.

"Hi-ya, Ferdinand, I'm Ferdinand," he said. "No, just kidding. I'm a manufacturer by trade, but now I'm a regulator — and somewhat of a celebrity, if I do say so myself!"

Ferdinand spoke hoarsely from the floor. "Hi. Pleased to meet—" Before he could finish, he gasped and closed his eyes.

The man moved closer. As soon as Ferdinand could feel the man's breath, he smashed a massive head butt into the look-alike's face, driving him onto his back and onto the floor of the cage.

Ferdinand hopped to his knees and drove his shins into the neck of the man, who was now gasping for air. The maneuver successfully pinned the man, making it nearly impossible for him to breathe.

"Untie me!" Ferdinand ordered. "Untie me now!"

Ferdinand pressed down with his shins harder and harder until all of the man's oxygen was cut off. He waited for almost a full minute before lightly easing up on the pressure. The man reached up, weakly, and worked at the knots.

"Faster!" Ferdinand barked.

The man worked at the knots until Ferdinand's hands were free. Ferdinand fell to his side and began to untie his own legs. The man beside him gasped for air.

When he was finished untying, Ferdinand jumped to his feet and struck the gasping man enormously hard in the head with his elbow, knocking him unconscious.

Ferdinand knew he had to work quickly. First, he stripped his look-alike of all clothing. Then he undressed as fast as he could, putting on the look-alike's baggies. Third, he redressed the unconscious man with his hemphouse uniform. Finally, he called for the guards.

The guards came and opened the cell. Ferdinand stepped freely from his cage, the crimson robes stuffed under his left arm.

"He asked me to give these to his girl," Ferdinand explained to the guard.

"Uh-huh," muttered the guards.

Ferdinand followed the guards through the hemphouse. When they reached the administration desk, Ferdinand checked out and walked freely into the evening air. Constant Love was across the parking lot, waiting for him in her car.

Ferdinand smiled and waved. He held up the robes and began jogging toward her. Ferdinand had cut the distance between them in half when, out of the blue, Big Stick Hun pulled into the parking lot.

Spotting Big Stick, Constant Love screamed, "Ferdinand!"

Ferdinand turned, spotted Big Stick's car, and began running. Big

Stick exited his car and emptied his handgun in Ferdinand's direction. Ferdinand reached the car and Constant slid over to the passenger seat. Big Stick was running toward them. Ferdinand fired the engine and screeched out of the parking lot. Big Stick dove for the car but missed. By the time he returned to fetch his own vehicle, they were gone.

By instinct alone, Ferdinand drove the car along the edge of the inner sanctum, toward the Southside Morgue.

"Where to now?" asked Constant Love.

"I'm heading to the morgue — on the Southside."

"Why?" she asked.

"I've been hit in the stomach ... here," Ferdinand said, opening his coat and displaying his blood-soaked shirt for the first time."

It was apparent that the wound was a mortal one.

"No!" screamed Constant Love. "No, Ferdinand. I won't let you die!"

Ferdinand looked down at himself. He hoarsely whispered, "I'm going to die, baby."

"No. No! Damn it! I won't allow it, Ferdinand!"

Ferdinand pulled the car over to the side of the road. They were on the outskirts of town, east of the inner sanctum. They were completely alone.

Constant Love held Ferdinand in her arms. She rocked him slowly.

"Ferdinand, we can make this. We can make the Southside Morgue."

"Not a chance," said Ferdinand. "Look at the blood I've lost. It would take us forty minutes from here, easily. And then they'd only catch me and catapult me into the great unknown."

Constant Love sobbed, holding and rocking Ferdinand.

"Thanks for the robes," he said. "You know, it's funny. All this time, I've been trying to escape — to get out of this madness. I've been thinking about those musicians ... and that poor soul out there in the Outlands. Those guys still dream, Love. Right here. Those hapless band guys right here in the inner sanctum. They were artists, you know. No regulations, no rules, no offices, no phones, or fax machines, or compuboxes, or deadlines. No working until they die with two weeks off every year until retirement. No forced labor. They created. That was enough. That made them free, even in this mad world."

Constant Love only held him.

"And another thing. You wouldn't believe it —"

Ferdinand stopped midsentence, coughing. He fell back weakly. She held him tightly.

"Just today, *today*, for the first time, I was thinking about children. Really, about a single child. Like I finally understood that connection and wanted it. That relationship. It's as if that child already exists and I'm just now recognizing its arrival."

"Ferdinand, I'm pregnant."

Ferdinand turned to look at Constant Love in renewed amazement. He mouthed the words, but no sound came out.

"When? How?" he asked.

"That time in your hovel ... with everyone outside," she said.

"That's amazing. You didn't use protection?" he asked.

"Never needed to," she said.

"What about Big Stick?"

"He's impotent," she said.

Ferdinand laughed loudly, and then coughed. "Poor Penelope!"

"I'm going to name it Theodore Axehandle, after you, Ferdinand."

"How do you know it's a boy?"

"I checked it out with the technicians. I wasn't going to have it if it was a girl. I didn't want it to grow up and be like me."

Ferdinand turned to stare at Constant Love again. His eyes gleamed with a combination of pride and astonishment.

"I don't want you ever, ever to feel that way again, do you hear me?" he said.

"You're the one, Ferdinand. You're the one who made me good again."

"Bullshit," he said. "All of my inspiration came from you. All of it."

Ferdinand hacked and coughed. Blood splattered from his mouth and onto the dashboard.

"I want him to know me, Love. I want him to know that his father didn't die in vain. I want him to know my story."

"He will, baby. I promise you. Abbot's already promised me he'll get him a job as a ranger."

Ferdinand laughed, weakly. "Is that what the winking was all about? He doesn't need to be a fucking ranger keeping post at that terrible wall or protecting us from the interlopers. Besides, there are no interlopers. We're the interlopers! Just let him be free, let him never forget who he is. I'll know him as a child. I'll know him as an artist."

Ferdinand doubled over. Constant Love held onto him tightly and pulled him close again.

"Don't go!" she cried. "Don't you go, Ferdinand."

Ferdinand lay still for a long moment. Then he opened his eyes once more to look at her.

"Bonvoyage, Ferdinand! You saw it! You saw it," she said. "Was it beautiful?"

Ferdinand's eyes were soft and they stared far away into the distant heavens. "It's so beautiful," he said.

~

The end.

Made in the USA
San Bernardino,
CA